WHITE RIVER MONSTER

KEITH ROMMEL

HELLBENDER BOOKS

an imprint of Sunbury Press, Inc.
Mechanicsburg, PA USA

HELLBENDER BOOKS

an imprint of Sunbury Press, Inc.
Mechanicsburg, PA USA

For information about special discounts for bulk purchases, please contact Sunbury Press Orders Dept. at (855) 338-8359 or orders@sunburypress.com.

To request one of our authors for speaking engagements or book signings, please contact Sunbury Press Publicity Dept. at publicity@sunburypress.com.

ISBN: 978-1-62006-721-5 (Trade paperback)

FIRST HELLBENDER BOOKS EDITION: Apri 2018

Product of the United States of America
0 1 1 2 3 5 8 13 21 34 55

Set in Bookman Old Style
Designed by Crystal Devine
Cover by Lawrence Knorr
Cover Art by Stephen Cooney
Edited by Jennifer Cappello

Continue the Enlightenment!

INSPIRED BY
THE LEGEND
OF THE
WHITE RIVER MONSTER.
NEWPORT. ARKANSAS.

In Memory of Marty Mallow

1

ARRIVAL

The taxi rumbled down a dirt road and jostled David Alan around in the back seat. He looked out the side window and for the past mile or two all he could see was a forest on either side of the vehicle and thick vegetation that made it seem impassible.

He was just about to question his driver he knew as Johnny where the river was when he said, "If you look out the left side, you're going to see the river any second," Johnny said. The man was so big, his body wobbled instead of bounced and the steering wheel rubbed his belly. The man with the thick southern accent had been nice enough during the long trip through winding back roads that had small hills and steep dips to see the White River. Sure enough, when he looked, he could see the fast moving river and white caps. Excitement made his chest flutter.

David stared in awe over the river and as fast as it came into sight, it disappeared behind another cluster of trees. He leaned back and held onto a smile. He was finally here. After enduring over 1,200 miles and 19 hours to get to the White River in Arkansas, he was aching to see what he travelled all this way for.

"Are you sure you want to do this?" Johnny asked.

"Yeah, I'm sure," David said. "I didn't travel all this way to turn around now."

"I suggest turning around," Johnny said and stared at David in the rearview mirror. David noticed him.

"Why is that?"

"Well, it would be for the same reason why I told you when I first picked you up. You're going to be alone in pitch black and it's freezing out there. If you happen to stumble on this monster you're seeking, he might not be nice."

"Alleged monster," David said. "I thank you for your concern, but I'm sure I'll be alright. I packed plenty of gear. At the very least, it's enough to last me two or three days."

"OK," Johnny said and pulled the cab to the side of the dirt road. "You refuse to listen and now I held up my end of the bargain. We're here."

David looked around and could only see forest. He kicked open the back door and could hear the sounds of the rapids. The trunk popped open and David retrieved his backpack and put it on. He slammed down the trunk to make sure it closed and he went to the driver's side door. Johnny rolled down the window.

"I wish you luck."

"Thank you," David said and paid what he owed.

"Now you're going to need to follow this path here all the way down to the water's edge. You're going to need to head that way," Johnny said and pointed in the direction he wanted David to go.

"OK," David said and looked at the path Johnny wanted him to travel. It was a steep drop off, but matted down from years of people using it to gain access to the river. "I want to thank you."

"Before you go I'd like to tell you something David."

"What's that?" David said and leaned on the car door to take off some of the weight.

"Do you know what a good Yankee is?"

"No Johnny, tell me, what's a good Yankee?"

"One that goes home," Johnny said and slapped his steering wheel with a laugh. His belly jiggled and

David laughed along right with him. "But for real. Be careful out there."

"I will."

Without pausing another moment, David started to walk the path but found his feet were sliding down the hard packed earth. He started to fall but used his hand to help him skate to the bottom of the incline. That's when everything opened up and David could see the White River speeding by him. The waves were small but violent and the movement of the water was swift. He made a mental note not to get too close to the water's edge and chance falling in. He couldn't swim real well and with the weight of his backpack, he'd sink to the bottom for sure. He didn't even want to think about the cold that would surely be awaiting him.

Investigation is what drove David Alan to Newport Arkansas in search of a local legend called the White River Monster. While doing some random research to find his next big freelance project, he had stumbled on an article dated back into the 1970's.

Each article he read contradicted the other and this only intensified his curiosity and compelled him to investigate the claims. It was tactful for the people that were trying to conceal the truth among phony sightings and descriptions that were most likely put out to pull people off the trail of the monster. David wasn't fooled by the breadcrumbs and morsels left behind in articles and interviews. He was much too smart for that, or so he believed.

But that elusive truth . . . it was somewhere out there and he intended on finding it. He was hoping to score some physical or visual evidence of the creature. He knew if he were to crack this story it would give him a push into becoming a staff newspaper writer instead of a freelancer running around in circles in search of something that might help him move up the ladder. He was so hungry for this dream of his to happen, that he used his vacation time to do this. A small bundle of money he saved for something special.

When he got a checklist from the internet and packed his backpack, he left the big city of New York with big hopes in mind. His spirit was high and he believed in his uncanny ability to unearth the impossible. He had no idea the beauty that awaited him when he arrived at the shoreline of the White River. When he descended that slope and looked up, natures beauty was all he could see.

The streets of New York were flooded with the sounds of impatience and annoyance and ran at a breakneck speed that never went away. There was like this constant hum of rats running a race they could never hope to win.

Here, right where he stood, he enjoyed the sound of the running winding river and the shaking of the thick outlying trees that served as a barrier to preserve its secrets.

He didn't know if he knew how to relax but he would try any chance he got. Having never been out of the city David had expected things to be different here and prepared as best he could with a hiking backpack stuffed with clothing, food, dishware, a fire starter, tent and a sleeping bag. He knew there wasn't going to be a corner store where he could buy a Pepsi and a freshly made sandwich. It was just him and the great outdoors.

As he continued his journey alongside the river, he couldn't help but acknowledge his admiration for the people that had settled in the houses not too far from the riverbank. Some were hidden well within the foliage and others poked out as if it liked to watch the flow of the river. The peacefulness of the area must take some getting used to and he could see how the locals might be annoyed when the rumors of a river monster started to surface again. Media and curious people from all walks of life descended on them in the early 1970s.

The legend first started in January of 1937 and interest in the creature waned until the big pop of the 1970s. There was no doubt people would come nosing around every now and then—like he was doing now—but for the most part, the legend had gone quiet. That made him all the more interested and he could feel the opportunity deep in his bones.

The creature was said to be nothing more than an Elephant Seal according to a crypto zoologist and biologist. David read all about the impossibility of that theory. How could the Elephant Seal come to be in the Mississippi through The Gulf of Mexico? The North Atlantic has no Elephant Seal population. Plain and simple, that was a decoy explanation. A copout when one doesn't have a reasonable explanation to provide to the public.

Rumors as to what the creature looked like ranged from a nasty looking fish to an apelike creature. It was able to travel on the land for a short period of time, standing upright and it was strong enough to bend trees as it descended from the forest and into the river.

A pale blue house with smoke billowing from its chimney was the first accessible cabin he came across since he started his journey some 10 miles upstream. Set back about twenty yards from the running water, he was unsure if his questioning would be welcomed. He decided before he even left New York to try and get the opinion of the locals.

Pulling his knit hat tight around his numbing ears, he huffed and watched his breath swirl around in the cold air. Lumbering up three wooden steps, he removed his gloves and knocked on the door. It was like pounding on brick and that hurt.

Only seconds went by and the front door swung open and a woman that wore a look of distaste stared at him.

"We're not interested in whatever it is you're selling," she said. "We have everything we need right here."

She started to close the door.

"I'm not here to sell you anything ma'am," David said. "I've come a long way to learn about the monster that is said to live in the river."

The woman pulled the door open and tugged on her chin. After a long moment of contemplation, she looked over her shoulder. "Hey Nick, we have another visitor." She looked at David. "What are you a reporter or something?"

"I am a freelance writer ma'am," he said and looked at the man that came up from behind his wife. "Hello sir, I'm David Alan."

The man stepped past his wife. "Well don't just stand there out in the cold. Come inside and get yourself warm. I have a fire going."

David accepted the invitation and stepped inside the house that smelled of stew. A crackling fire raged in the fireplace and a wooden table and chairs that were probably handmade was only a few feet inside the quaint home. Beyond where he stood, a living room with a simple couch, loveseat, side table and lamp didn't do much to hold his attention.

"Please sit," the man said and David did. "This is my wife Marsha and I'm sure you heard her call me. My name is Nick . . . Nick Flowers."

"Thank you for your hospitality sir," David said and took off his pack and set it down by his side. "It is quite cold out there. Colder than I expected."

"There's a bite to the air that'll go right through ya," Marsha said and placed a stack of hot rolls in front of the men. "It's our pleasure to have you as a guest. So please, have some rolls they're nice and hot."

David smiled. "Thank you."

"What can I do for you David?"

David took a bite out of the roll and it was warm and buttery. "Thank you, this is good." He held up the roll.

"Homemade."

"It's wonderful, thank you."

"We haven't had a writer come out here in quite some time."

"I've been reading the articles online and it really made me curious as to how many contradicting articles were available. I'm here seeking the truth about the White River Monster."

Nick chuckled and covered his mouth to help stifle the outburst. "I'm sorry, I don't mean to be rude. I hate that you travelled all the way here from the sound of your accent maybe New York?"

"Yes."

"Well, you came here for a legend that grew to a fever pitch in the 1970s. You need to know it was all for nothing. The stories you read are just stories. People looking to make a buck. I mean you had all of these people here . . . it looked like a circus . . . and not one good picture. No tangible evidence. There were just stories made up and all that did was stir the hornets' nest."

"I appreciate your honesty Mr. Flowers. I am going to camp at the riverbed tonight where the alleged sightings took place. Although I'm not too clear where that is, I'll find a suitable spot. I'd like to see what I can capture. A strange sound . . . maybe a disturbance in the water. Something."

"I want to warn you that it's going to get really cold out there tonight. Are you sure you want to do that? If you decide against it, we have a spare room where you can stay until morning. At least you will be fed and have a warm place to put your head."

"Thank you for the offer but I didn't come all this way to be chased away by the cold. Being a freelancer, I have to come away with a story . . . even if there is no story. Reporting the truth is what I do for a living. So I have to do it and hope I can sell whatever it is I find."

"I completely understand."

"Forgive me if I'm treading on grounds you're not comfortable with. Do you know where the spot is? The place I am most likely to spot the monster?" David paused in thought for a moment. "Please allow me to change that question. If you thought the legend was real and you wanted to try and collect evidence, where would the best place for me to go and spend the night?"

"I'm no expert on a monster that doesn't exist David, but I can tell you exactly where that spot is you're seeking."

"That would be appreciated."

"In fact you're really close," Mr. Flowers said and pointed. "About a half to three quarters of a mile up river that way, you're going to see a horseshoe shaped cutout in the trees by the shoreline." He rested his elbows on the table. "Make your camp there. Hopefully you'll find something of interest that'll help you with that article of yours."

"Thank you Mr. Flowers."

He sat back. "No problem at all. Before you set off, please have something more to eat."

David stood up and grabbed his pack. "I appreciate the offer, but that roll was satisfying and I'd like to have camp set up before night begins to fall. I'm not much of an outdoorsman and won't pretend to be. I need every second of daylight I can save."

"Very well," Nick said and patted David on the shoulder. "I wish you well and if you need to stop by in the morning to warm up, please knock. You're more than welcome."

"Thank you," David said and left the house. He couldn't imagine someone doing that in New York and getting the same response he had just gotten. Although it was just a stereotype for the most part, he could imagine being hollered at or even assaulted for bothering someone. But here, in Arkansas, things were much different besides a southern accent. The people seemed genuinely kind and even outgoing.

David walked along the riverbank, going the direction Mr. Flowers had told him. The cold nipped at his skin and the sweat that had his shirt wet hugged him in a cold embrace that only added to his chill. He started to shiver.

A quarter of a mile through his journey, he came by another house. A male and a female were outside, splitting wood when they took notice of him.

"Hey!" The man shouted and dropped the ax he was swinging only moments ago. "You're on private property."

David stopped and raised his hands to try and defuse the situation. "I'm sorry, I didn't know. I just came from the Flowers residents and he directed me this way."

"They did, did they?"

"Yes sir."

The man had rosy cheeks from the cold and his eyes were pulled down in a scowl.

"Damn neighbors of mine." He shook his head. "Did they tell you to go to the cutout to see Whitey?"

"I'm sorry, who?"

"Whitey. The White River Monster. That's what we call him around here."

"Yes sir that is where he told me to go."

The man shook his head. "You should know the legend before you try and stick your nose in it. You people keep crawling out of the woodwork and disturb our way of life and for what?"

"I—"

"You what?"

"I don't want any trouble."

The man shook his head. "You come on private property, meander around as you please and make up tales that only bring more people here and you tell me you don't want any trouble?"

"I can offer you my apology and be on my way."

"Oh you can, can you?"

David nodded, his heart pumping, his eyes noticing the man hadn't stepped far away from the ax at all. His wife looked as mean as he was. Her face was pulled down into an expression of frostbitten annoyance.

"Let him be Rick," the woman said. "He looks like he's about to shit himself."

Rick laughed. "Yeah Joan, I noticed that, too."

David kept quiet and let them have their fun.

"Do you think the Flowers warned him not to mess with Joan and Rick Hisster," Joan said. Rick's scowl cracked as his lips upturned into a smile.

"Go on then, get on your way," Rick said. "You're gonna freeze your ass off for nothing. You'll see."

David hurried away and didn't stop until he found the cutout Mr. Flowers had mentioned. He stood for a moment, winded, and looked at the bizarre clearing. It seemed manmade and all the surrounding trees had been cut down to stumps. The camping area was a near perfect eight by eight clearing that was ideal for someone looking to set up camp.

He dropped the heavy pack to the ground and with a tremble in his numb hands he set up the tent and gathered medium sized rocks off the riverbank. He made a small fire pit as far away from the tent as he could and gathered a bushel of twigs and sticks that would be enough to get him through the night if he needed to keep the fire lit.

His focus moved to his equipment delicately packed in the backpack. The first thing he did was check the batteries and the replacements on his night vision camera that could take both still pictures and film. Satisfied he was ready for the night and hopeful he wouldn't run into the Hisster's ever again, he grabbed a pot and a can of beans and started on dinner.

The Hisster's had left quite the impression and he actually felt vulnerable letting them know where he was staying the night. He would have to be vigilant and make sure they didn't do anything to impede on his investigation and try to harm him in any way. Maybe they were the White River Monster.

2

THE WHITE RIVER

Night had fallen on the White River and with it, a stiff penetrating cold. Sitting next to the fire to stay warm, David had a full belly and found both the crackle of the fire and the sound of the river flowing to be soothing. It sure beat the bustle of cars speeding from light to light and the fray of taxi cab drivers that enjoyed scaring you from light to light. The people that chattered on their cell phones were endless. Just to see them holler at one another for something meaningless and petty. They showed no regard for one another and only cared about coming in first.

David took control of his FLIR night vision camera and began to scour the shoreline for any signs of abnormalities in the water around him. The talk Mr. Flowers gave him made him feel as though that most of the night would consist of nothing but some fish jumping here and there and maybe a sound coming from the woods from a curious animal drawn in by his scent. If he were lucky.

But he would try anyway. It was what he came to do and he took this trip as he did every account that he read about the White River Monster seriously.

Besides the chill and the foreign sounds, he reminded himself that being out here was hardly any different than being in his apartment. Alone was the way he did things since his divorce. He was better off. That way he couldn't get hurt ever again.

Pushing those thoughts aside, David approached the shoreline and scanned the camera as far as he could see to the left and right of where he was staying. Watching the small LED screen, he didn't see anything out of the ordinary. Hungry to find something more than crackling sticks being devoured by a fire and the freezing cold that attacked him when he stepped away from it, he began to wander the riverbank. He purposely ventured in the opposite direction of the Hisster's home.

He continued to search, and at times, cut the camera and used his natural senses to see if he could hear anything that might require his attention. A big boulder invited him to sit and rest and he spent another hour there, shaking at the wind that scraped his exposed face. He went through two batteries and hours of footage before he decided to call it quits and return to camp.

Placing another fresh battery in the camera, dawn wasn't too far off and he decided to get a few hours of sleep before he packed up camp and returned the way he came. That was the only way he knew.

"I see the Hisster's are going to be my only obstacle instead of some monster that occupies the river around here," he said into the comfort of his tent. Remaining dressed he slipped into his North Face sleeping bag and kept his camera close at his side. Just in case. "I'll have to run past them as quickly as possible tomorrow." He laughed. "Yeah, I can do that. My feet are frozen and my body is stiff from the long hike in. The bright side is my pack will be a bit lighter after emptying out some of the food containers I brought."

His eyes felt heavy and the natural darkness that came with sleep began to close in on him. His body twitched and his breathing fell into a low, rhythmic beat.

Crack.

David's eyes snapped open and he listened, unsure if what he heard was something made from his sleeping mind or if it was something outside his tent.

Crack.

The sound was close enough that his skin goosed and it wasn't brought on by the cold either. He no longer felt the chill and grabbed his camera and powered it up. Nervous fingers pinched the zipper on the mosquito netting and as quietly as possible, he unzipped it and looked through the LED display on his camera to try and locate the source of the noise.

His body turned warm and his lower half cemented to the ground when he hit the heat signature. His thumb fumbled to hit the video record button but instead he changed the setting to take individual pictures.

A tall man . . . no, it was far too big to be a man . . . it was a creature and it was in the brush about five feet away from his camp. It was huge and hard to see with the naked eye because it was dark in color and it blended with the tint of morning. Maybe the skin was black or gray; it was hard to tell in this light. His heart gave the inside of his ribcage a beating and fear and indecision made him unsure.

He looked into the display on the camera once again and snapped a picture. He looked back into the brush and the creature was gone.

Crack.

His eyes swung towards the riverbed and the camera followed and what he didn't realize was he had been snapping pictures the entire time. His eyes grew wide and his body turned numb as he watched the giant creature step into the shallow water and settle down on its belly. It slid into the water and the wake it created was huge. The water washed up near his tent and the hot embers that remained in the fire pit sizzled as they died.

David remained on his knees and looked through the display and panned the water. He tried to find what he had just seen but there was no trace. Whatever it was, it was huge and it was gone as soon as it appeared.

He sat back on his heels and with quivering hands he reviewed what he might have captured on the camera. To his surprise, he had some pictures as a heat signature that came across as a giant red smudge with no details other than the outline of an oddly shaped head. As he thumbed through the pictures with nervous excitement he found pictures where the camera had changed to taking pictures without the use of infrared. Some of the detail that could be seen was amazing. The light of dawn was perfect. The first picture was of its legs. They were hairy and the feet had what appeared to be three toes and possibly webbed. The next picture was so eerie that David couldn't look at what he was seeing at first. It scared him to know that thing was so close to him and that it seemed to come when he was no longer active. It had intelligence. That thought compounded with the evidence he caught was enough to chase him out. He didn't want to be here in this small clearing any longer. In fact, he longed for the city life and never wanted to return to the country. It was a mistake coming here.

In one of the photographs the creature had been looking right at him with eyes that were set close together and a nose that was two pin holes. The thin face with a snapping turtle like beak and gnarled teeth that protruded made him shiver.

The need to get out of there outweighed the fear that held him captive only moments ago. Survival mode kicked in and he worked as fast as he could to pack camp. Whatever the hell that thing was, he wanted nothing to do with it. Whatever lurked in those waters and came ashore to stalk things in the forest and possibly him was as scary as hell.

Shouldering his haphazardly packed backpack, he hurried out of there and didn't care that he was leaving some items behind.

EVIDENCE OF THE WHITE RIVER MONSTER

David ran past the Hisster's house without care that they might spot him. Onwards he pushed, sticking close to the riverbed, but not too close that the monster could easily reach out and yank him into the freezing cold water.

Short of breath and burning lungs, he paid no attention to it. He wanted to forget what he saw and get back to civilization and feel the safety in numbers; to be distracted by all the commotion that never stopped.

Stepping out from a cluster of trees, Mr. Flowers held onto a few freshly caught fish on a line. David collided with him and both men fell down. David smacked the back of his head off a tree and Mr. Flowers groaned as he pushed himself to his hands and knees.

"I'm sorry," David said. "I didn't see you there."

"You walloped me a good shot there David," Mr. Flowers said and was slow to stand. "This ground is as hard as a rock, too."

"I'm so sorry."

"What are you running so fast from?" Mr. Flowers said and extended a hand to help David to his feet. "Did the neighbors give you hell?"

"No, that's not why I was in a hurry."

"Well I thought you were investigating the monster that is supposed to live in these waters? Are you giving up already?"

"I was," David said and took Mr. Flowers hand and allowed the man to help him to his feet. He had hit his head so hard that he found he needed to lean against a tree to keep his balance. "But something spooked me and I'm not going back there."

"Probably some wild animal," Mr. Flowers said. "You look really unsteady. Why don't you hold onto my arm so you can keep your balance and come inside the house until you're feeling better?"

David tried to look over his shoulder but he became really dizzy and focused on Mr. Flowers. "I should go."

"You can't travel on foot while you're like this. You must have hit your head or something."

"I did," David said and rubbed the lump.

"I won't lie to you. You look like you've been scared shitless. You're safe here so try and calm down."

David nodded. "OK."

"You!' David heard from behind and turned to look. His head was still swimming. "You don't think I saw you running through my property when I told you not to?" Mr. Hisster said with his angry wife in tow.

"Take it easy on him Rick," Mr. Flowers said. "Something spooked him and he was running from the camping spot. He just ran into me and smacked his head pretty good off a tree. The damn clunk was so loud that I can't believe he's still conscious."

"Good, it serves him right," Joan Hisster said.

Marsha Flowers came out of the house and quickly approached the unruly assembly. "What's going on here?"

"Trespassing is what's going on," Joan said. "And you two sent him that way. Why would you do that when you know we don't like people like him around here?"

"Because he was curious," Marsha said. "And he wouldn't stop until he cursed that curiosity. He seemed like a nice enough guy when he first came by so why don't you give him a break?"

"Besides, it's not like he was going to find anything," Nick Flowers said. "We both know that."

"I found something," David whispered with his headache pounding deep inside his skull.

"What did you find?" Rick Hisster asked with a smile.

"Mr. Flowers, if you don't mind I'd like to take you up on your offer and get inside your house. I'm not feeling that great."

"Sure David, come on inside," Nick said. He looked at Joan and Rick. "You two can come if you can behave yourself and forgive the young man for running across your yard."

Joan and Rick looked at each other. "That's fine," Rick said.

"You two act like you live on sacred ground."

"It's my damn property!"

"Just forget it," Marsha said. "Let's tend to him." They all went into the house and sat at the table.

"I have to show you this," David said and took out his FLIR camera. His hands shook as he showed the group the pictures he had captured.

"Photoshop is an amazing thing," Joan said. "Here we go with the damn circus again. Come on Rick, let's get out of here. I told you this guy was trouble."

"I didn't Photoshop anything," David said.

The couple left, ignoring him.

"These pictures are real," David reiterated.

"I know," Nick said. "That's Whitey."

David swallowed hard. "Are you saying I caught a glimpse of The White River monster?"

Nick nodded, his expression somber. "You did and it looks like a good one, too."

David smiled and then laughed. "Ouch," he said and grabbed his head. The laugh was more from nerves rather than a celebration.

"We can't let these pictures get out there," Nick Flowers said.

"I'm sorry?"

"It's just a legend and it needs to stay that way." Marsha said.

"But what I captured is important on so many different levels. It shows a species never captured on film before. It proves some of those people actually saw something."

"It doesn't matter," Nick said. "Those pictures of yours just don't exist."

David didn't like the change of mood and although his head still hurt something awful, he had a feeling that he needed to get out of there.

"What paper do you write for?" Nick said.

"Whatever one is paying for my article."

"Oh yeah, you're a freelancer, that's right."

"Yes."

Nick shook his head. "I don't think anyone knows you're here, do they?"

David stood on unsteady legs. "Of course people know I'm here."

"Now David . . ."

"I think I should go. Thank you for your hospitality."

"I think you realize that I can't allow you to go."

"Well no matter what you say, I'm leaving."

Marsha came up behind David with a wrought iron skillet and hit him in the back of the head. He fell to the floor in a heavy heap.

4

THE MONSTER

David's eyes had a hard time opening. He could feel the blood that had soaked his shirt and ran down his face had dried. The headache had become so intense just thinking hurt and the cold was so intense it seemed to seep all the way into his bones.

He tried to move but couldn't. He had been bound to a tree next to the campsite he abandoned. Marsha and Nick checked the knots and stepped back and looked at David.

"What's happening?" David said. "Why am I here?"

"You've been chosen," Marsha said.

"Whitey only shows himself to the ones he wants," Nick said.

David pulled against the rope that bound him. There was no play in the rope and the knots were firm and unbreakable.

"Once you captured him on film, your fate was sealed," Nick said.

"My running into you wasn't an accident then, was it?"

Marsha and Nick laughed together. "That a boy. No, of course it wasn't."

"Please let me go. You can have the footage and I won't tell anyone what happened here, I swear it."

"I'm sure you mean that right now," Marsha said. "But we know what would happen once you got back to your big city with people waving money around to get the exclusive. We just cannot allow that. The legend needs to remain a legend."

"It was nice knowing you David," Nick said. "I actually thought you were a nice guy and hoped it didn't come to this. But we have to protect what is ours. I'm sure you understand."

"No I don't," David said. "Please just let me go."

Marsha and Nick walked away, arm in arm and didn't look back. David remained attached to the tree for hours, his eyes fixated on the river where the monster had returned to the water. Soon sleep came and his head slumped forward and the comfort of sleep took away his worry.

A cold hand gripped his chin, jarring David awake. He looked into the eyes of the monster he had photographed. Pain in his head and the cloudiness of being torn from sleep combined with a sudden all encompassing fear gripped him.

The webbed fingers were powerful and they turned his head from side to side. Whitey gurgled and went nose to nose with him. The creature smelled like the deep, bringing bile into his mouth. It stood upright and David managed to gauge the creature to be eight feet tall or better.

It bent again, seeming curious. The eyes that studied him were animalistic. The mouth with the odd beaklike shape and gnarled teeth opened and snapped shut; the teeth gnashed together and David turned his head away and pressed his body as flat as he could against the tree. The skin had fins and tentacles and appeared slimy and the massive body looked like it belonged in the hominid family but the frightening deformities might put it in the amphibian family.

The creature grunted and wrapped one crushing hand around David's head and the other hand grabbed his legs. The creature pulled and the strain on David's innards from the rope digging into his abdomen was tremendous. His eyes bulged and felt

like they were going to pop out of his head. He tried
to scream but the air was forced out of his lungs.
The creature pulled, seeming to use very little of its
might and the rope sliced through David's body with
ease and his spine snapped, his body torn him in
two. The blood drained out of his body and stained
the shoreline as the creature held onto both parts of
the body and dragged it to the water.

The beast went onto its belly and slithered into
the water, dragging David underwater with him. The
beast swam away and dove deep with very few
knowing of his real existence.

5

DAVID'S APARTMENT

Taegan Alan hadn't heard from his brother,
David, in about a week. At first, Taegan thought
David might be caught up with his freelance work
when he didn't get his normal call at the beginning
of the week. But when he didn't get a call toward
the end of the week either, Taegan tried calling his
brother multiple times. Every time he called, his
brother's phone went right to voicemail, which gave
Taegan a bad feeling he couldn't shake.

It was unlike his brother not to communicate,
especially since his divorce. His ex-wife was
impossible and drove a wedge between them, but
once David broke free of her oppression their
brotherly relationship improved dramatically. They
shared fond stories of their childhood and memories
of their now deceased parents. David often
complimented Taegan's wife and Taegan's ability to
pick the sweet ones. Taegan told David he would
meet someone new, someone better, that he had to
be patient. David said he wasn't interested, and his
words sounded convincing.

The lack of communication was what brought
Taegan to his brother's apartment. First, he was
looking to make sure he was all right. When he
entered the apartment, he was nervous he might find
him sprawled out on the floor. Taegan had heard of
that happening so many times. When he found the
apartment empty and dark, he realized he needed to
find a clue as to where his brother might have gone.

Taegan turned on every light in the apartment so
that he didn't miss a thing. A desk in the corner of

the bedroom had stacks of papers on it, and the possibility of information drew him over there. Page by page, he flipped through and only found haphazard ideas for future articles scribbled down among unpaid bills. A trash can next to the desk invited Taegan to look. Crumpled papers revealed the same things as the top of the desk. He stood with a sigh.

"Where did you go, David? What are you up to, and why didn't you tell me?"

That's when he saw a closed laptop on the unmade bed, half covered by the crumpled blanket. He took it out, opened it, and pressed the power button. The computer booted up, and Taegan rested on the edge of the bed and waited for the Windows screen to open. When it did, Google Chrome was already open, and the page it was on was Wikipedia. Strangely, it was about something called "The White River Monster," located in Newport, Arkansas. It was a legend, a thing of imagination, and it appeared his brother had a great interest in it.

His theory was proven right when Taegan checked the history on the computer. Search after search had to do with the White River Monster and the multiple sightings of it that had taken place for over a century. This legend had started in the early 1900s. It spoke about the wave of people who had descended on Newport, but Taegan didn't care about those details. He was looking for something that might help him find his brother.

Curious, he searched the history a bit more carefully, scrolling through and reading each hit. Right in the middle of his studying this monster, there was a hit on Amazon. Taegan navigated to his brother's Gmail inbox and found a confirmation receipt email pertaining to some camping supplies he had purchased. The list was rather simple: a tent, large backpack, boots, gloves, hat, coat, a pot, fire starters, and even a stainless steel cup with a moose embossed on the side. Maybe his brother was getting tired of the city life and was looking to get out into the country. What it must be like to smell the fresh country air instead of exhaust.

Navigating back through the history, Taegan scrolled some more. David had purchased an airline ticket that would take him into Portland and then another ticket that would take him from Portland to Newport Airport via Charter Harbor Air.

Taegan did some quick searches on Google, found the information he needed, and booked his flights. He found a recent picture that was taken of him and his brother, stuffed that into his pocket, and rushed out of the apartment. He had enough time to get home and get his gloves and hat and anything else he could think of that he might need to protect himself from the bitter elements he knew he was about to face. He would also have to tell his wife, Melinda, everything he knew and what he was about to do.

6

NEWPORT, ARKANSAS

After the second leg of the flight, Taegan finally arrived in Newport, Arkansas. Hailing a cab, he jumped into the back seat and shivered at the slicing winds that went right through his winter clothing.

"Man, it's freezing out there," he said and rubbed his gloved hands together.

"So what brings you to Arkansas?" the cab driver asked and looked at Taegan in the rearview mirror.

Taegan looked out the window and glimpsed the bustle of the airport and couldn't help but compare it to the flurry of New York City. There was just no comparison. He lived in the craziest, most expensive and overpopulated place in America. If his brother was looking to move to the country maybe he had the right idea.

"Have you heard of the White River Monster?" Taegan asked.

"Well," the cab driver said and turned his eyes to the road. "I think everyone who lives around these parts hears about the monster since about the age of four. The legend is well known and quite popular with the kids. You should see Halloween around here."

"Can I show you a picture of someone?"

"Sure," the driver said and reached a hand back. Taegan placed the picture he'd brought into the man's hand. "Can you tell me if you recognize that man with me?"

"I can't say that I do," the driver said and held it out for Taegan to take back.

"Are you sure?"

"As sure as I can be. Where to?"

"Just drive, if you don't mind?"

"Of course." The driver moved through the streets with ease. "But keep in mind that the doors on this vehicle are like a revolving door. I like to picture it as one of those fancy ones in the big city hotels. I'm like a waiter, in a sense. I have to turn them tables so I can earn a living, do you know what I mean?"

"Yeah, I know exactly what you mean."

Taegan put the picture away.

"This may be a bit forward, but do you know where I might be able to find this monster?"

The driver chuckled. "You know that monster isn't real. That's why they call it a legend."

"I've read that some people believe it is real."

"Yeah, and some people believe Santa is real, too."

"I get that, but if the monster was real, where would someone go to look for him?"

"How do you it's a him?"

"OK. *It.*"

The driver laughed. "I'm only teasing."

Taegan wasn't in the mood for jokes.

The driver's gaze flashed in the rearview mirror again but quickly went back to the road. "Listen, there's this other cabbie named Johnny Phatz. His last name is just a nickname; I don't know his real name. He's had it as long as I've known him, and that's how he introduces himself. Anyhow, if there was one iota of truth to this White River Monster, he would know where to take you."

"Thank you for telling me that. I can't tell you how important it is that I meet with him. I'll pay you extra if you take me to see Johnny."

The cabbie sat quiet for a minute, and it felt like an eternity to Taegan. He hated the silence and wondered what there was to think about. The only logical thought would be Johnny does know where to go and he's not willing to show it to just anybody.

"How much more are you willing to pay?"

"On top of the fare I'll give you an extra fifty."

The cabbie thought some more. Taegan was confident he was going to bite. To imagine he had just arrived in Newport and he had already nailed his first big break to finding his brother was more than a pound of luck.

"Let me call him and see what he says," the cabbie said and looked at Taegan in the rearview mirror. "I'll see what I can do, but I can't make any promises."

"Thank you," Taegan said and tried to contain his excitement. His outward demeanor was collected, calm, and curious of his surroundings. But inside he was jumping for joy, and he wanted to scream out in praise because this was the break he needed.

7

CONTACT

Taegan paid the driver his fare and handed him the extra fifty.

"Hell," the cabbie said. "I would have done it for an extra twenty."

Taegan exited the cab and immediately spotted Johnny Phatz. He was a massive man; tall with a belly that hung over his belt. He leaned on the driver's side door and watched Taegan approach with his arms folded across his chest.

"Hello, Johnny, my name is Taegan." He extended a hand and Johnny shook it. His grip was unbelievably strong, even though it appeared that he was trying to be gentle. "I was told that you were the man who would know where to take me if I wanted to spot the White River Monster."

Johnny sighed. "It's a legend, you know that?"

"That's what I've been told."

"So why seek it out when you know there's nothing there?"

"Let's just say I have an aching curiosity. If you take me, I'll pay double the fare, whatever it is. No questions asked."

Johnny raised a brow and chuckled. "Well, I guess you found what shuts me up rather quickly."

Taegan shrugged. "Money can be a great motivator."

"All right then, get in."

Taegan got in the back seat of the cab and Johnny squeezed himself behind the steering wheel. The taxi's engine revved to life and the driver pressed the gas pedal.

"So you said you have an aching curiosity. You're going to be heading through some rough terrain, and you come with nothing but heavy clothing. I don't know how pleasant your journey is going to be."

"I'll be fine," Taegan said, his motivation coming from the need to find his brother. That impulse was sharper than a knife and anyone's stamina.

"If you say so," Johnny said, and the cab lurched forward. "I've got to make up some time. Night is coming soon, and you don't want to be making that journey in the dark. Some of the bypass is treacherous. All it takes is one out of place rock that you don't see and you twist and ankle and you're all alone."

Taegan grabbed his pocket and felt reassured that he had his cell phone. There was no sense in debating the unimportant things. He just wanted to get there.

"God forbid something worse happened . . . you'd find yourself in a world of trouble out there. There's an abundance of wildlife that this creature you seek could be living off of—as well as quite possibly anyone not strong enough to stand and defend themselves."

✤
DOWN THE RABBIT HOLE

Taegan and Johnny made it off of the paved road and onto a bumpy dirt road. They'd been traveling for miles, and Taegan was growing impatient. He was being bounced around and saw nothing but trees. He worked on getting his focus back to try to find something out of the ordinary. A morsel would do. The forest on either side of him all looked the same. There was a certain danger in that because he could easily get turned around. At first he hadn't, but now he appreciated Johnny's warning because it could very well save his life. He hoped his brother had received a similar word of caution.

Every now and then he'd get a glimpse of a river with white-capped rapids. He knew they were close to the White River. Soon the cab slowed to a stop.

"We're here," Johnny said.

Taegan could only see trees and was unsure where here actually was.

"Trust me, we're here," Johnny said. "I see that look all the time."

"OK," Taegan said and took the picture out of his pocket. "Do you mind looking at this picture before I go?"

"Sure."

Johnny took the photograph and studied it. He groaned and pulled at his wobbly chin.

"You know, I see hundreds of people in any given week. The faces start to blend together."

"Well, he would have had a thick New York accent like mine."

"Was he a reporter?"

"Yes!" Taegan said and his face lit up and his hope burned bright.

"Oh yes, now I remember him. He was a really nice guy, hell bent on finding proof of the monster. Like I do with everyone else who's looking for Whitey, I dropped him off right here. It had to be a week ago I think, maybe a bit longer."

"Is there anything else you can remember about him?"

"Yeah. He had this massive backpack like he was staying for a month. I knew he was out of his element, but I couldn't convince him to not go."

Johnny handed the picture back.

"Can you tell me what direction he went in?"

"Down this embankment here. Be careful. It's steep, and you're more than likely going to slide halfway down if not all the way down. Try to control your descent or you'll fall right into the river. This will take you next to the riverbank." Johnny pointed in the direction he wanted Taegan to go. "Keep heading that way. The walk is long, and remember to watch your footing."

"I can't thank you enough," Taegan said and paid Johnny as promised.

"Not a problem," Johnny said and stuffed the money into his breast pocket. "I appreciate the extra money. Things have been tight."

"It is the least I can do. Take care, Johnny."

"You too. Eyes open all the time."

Taegan slid down the steep embankment but didn't come close to getting wet. He began to travel in the direction Johnny told him with a chest and mind full of determination.

9

THE FLOWERS

Taegan felt like he had been traveling forever. His feet hurt and his back ached. He imagined his brother walking this same path with a large pack on his back and it amazed him.

Soon he came upon a couple who looked to be in their late fifties. They were collecting firewood for their cabin, which was set back from the river. Gray smoke plumed from the chimney and Taegan stared longingly; he needed to warm up in the worst way. He couldn't feel his face, hands, or feet. The sun was going down, and it felt like the temperature was dropping, too.

"Hello," the older man said.

"Hello," Taegan said in return.

"You look like the chill has seeped into your bones, young man. "Your face is red, and I can see you shivering from here."

Taegan nodded. "Your eyes don't fail you, sir. I've walked quite the distance."

"What brings you around this way?"

"I'm looking for the White River Monster."

"Well," the man said. "You're not the first to come this way, and you won't be the last. Although you are heading in the right direction, not one single person has come out with any proof."

"I don't know if I'm looking for proof of the monster."

The man raised a brow. "Then what are you after?"

"Right now?" Taegan said and shivered. "A little warmth would help."

"Right, how rude of me. My name is Nick Flowers, and this is my wife, Marsha. Why don't you come inside and warm up. I'm sure Marsha has something warm to give you."

"Thank you so much. I'm Taegan."

"What a unique name," Marsha said, and as a group they went into the cabin. The fire crackled and Taegan sat at a table next to it, putting out his hands to capture the warmth. He rubbed them together and offered the Flowers a smile. "Again, thank you both very much."

"You're welcome."

Marsha placed some hot rolls on the table and told Taegan to dig in. Without hesitation he took a roll and felt the warmth growing inside. He was hungry but hadn't want to stop; he wouldn't have, if not for the cold. He feared the fading light.

Once he was full and finished, he reached into his pocket and took the photograph out and slid it across the table to Nick Flowers. "Can you tell me if you've seen this man?"

Nick took the picture and looked at it.

"Hun?"

Marsha came over and looked at the picture. She nodded.

"Yeah, we've seen him," Nick said.

"He was passing through and had this large pack on his back," Marsha said.

"We invited him inside, but he declined. He was focused. I guess you could say he was a man on a mission."

"I don't know why he wouldn't accept our help," Marsha said. "It was as cold that day as it is right now."

"There was a taxicab driver who dropped me off about five miles back. He told me the man in the picture here was looking for the monster."

"He was probably heading for the cutout."

"The cutout?" Taegan asked.

"Yeah, it's only a little ways up in the direction you were heading. It is perfect for a campsite, and although I don't believe it, some people claim to have had sightings of the monster there."

"OK," Taegan said and stood. "Thank you. I think I should go there."

"Oh no," Marsha said and shook her head and placed a gentle hand on Taegan's shoulder. "Dusk has fallen now, and you will never find your way."

"She's right," Nick said.

"You're our guest now. Stay the night, and don't think anything about it. Get some breakfast in the morning and head out then."

Taegan thought about it only for a second because he remembered how biting the cold was. Besides, he knew it wasn't safe to travel a path like that with no light. He had lost his footing a few times and almost fell. Johnny's warning was fresh on his mind. "I appreciate your offer very much. Thank you. I agree that I could use a night to warm up and start fresh in the morning, as you say."

"Very good," Nick said.

"I'll ready your room then," Marsha said with a smile.

10

THE CUTOUT

"I want to thank you for such a wonderful meal," Taegan said.

"Think nothing of it," Marsha said.

"We don't get much company, so when Marsha is able to serve her meals to other people, she jumps at the chance. I guess she's a bit of a showoff."

"Nick!" Martha said and put her hands on her hips.

"How did you sleep?"

"Like a rock. Thank you for allowing me to stay."

"You're welcome."

"Well, I must be heading to the cutout to see if anyone is there," Taegan said.

Nick showed him out, and the blast of cold air that greeted Taegan went right through him. But he pressed on, continuing on the course he was told to travel. He passed a second house, but no one was home . . . or at least no one was outside gathering wood.

After about ten more minutes, he came upon the cutout the Flowers were referring to. It had to be it. The flat ground was perfect for a tent, and there were trees that had been cut down to stumps to help keep the area clear. It wasn't too far off the shoreline and gave access to an opening that would grant someone ample places to explore. Taegan scoured the area but saw no sign of a tent or a person having been there recently.

He sat on a stump and watched the rapids and thought it quite beautiful but distracting all the same. The chill kept biting him, nibbling at his skin like a million pinpricks. But he tried to pay it no attention and immerse himself into the thought of what might have happened to his brother.

"Maybe," Taegan said to the trees around him and the fast moving water. "Just maybe we crossed paths during transit. Maybe he's already back in his apartment in New York and I'm out here, virtually in the middle of nowhere, looking for someone who's not missing."

Taegan pulled out his cell phone and tried again to call David, but there was no reception. He stood and searched the area one last time. All he could find were undefined footprints in the mud, and he wasn't sure if they were his own or David's or belonging to someone else who might have spent a few nights here.

He resigned with a sigh, acknowledging the blisters on his feet and the cold that helped him cope with them. It was time for the long, dreaded walk back.

11

TRUTH AND LIES

Taegan used the river's edge to help guide him along the same way he came. If he were to use the trees he might get turned around so he knew the safest way back was to use the shoreline.

"Hey, trespasser!" a man yelled, and Taegan saw a man with a red face approaching him. "You're on private property! Didn't you see the signs with the bright orange letters on them nailed to the trees?"

"No, I didn't. But I'd like to offer my apology. I was at the cutout on the suggestion of the Flowers."

"Great, the damn neighbors again," the man said. He scowled and looked in the direction of the Flowers' cabin. "They cause me nothing but grief. I wish they would either die or move. I know that sounds harsh, but they've been a thorn in my side for years. They send all these people to that damn cutout."

"I didn't mean to upset you. I didn't know I was crossing private property."

"Well you are," the man snapped. "Learn to read. All of you damn monster chasers . . ."

"I want to make something clear. I didn't come here looking for the White River Monster."

"No?"

The man seemed intrigued and even appeared to calm a little.

Taegan withdrew the picture and held it out for the man to take. He stepped forward and took it and then stepped back, seeming unsure. Trust clearly wasn't his strongest trait.

"Have you seen that man?" Taegan said.

"Yes, I have. I even had a few run-ins with him. No longer than a week ago."

"Mister . . .?"

"The name is Rick. Rick Hisster."

"It's nice to meet you, Rick. I'm Taegan Alan. Can you tell me about the man you saw?"

"The Flowers took him in after he left the campsite. He stayed at that cutout for one night and hightailed it out of there. He was running away from there like his pants were on fire," Rick said. "I followed him because I wanted to let him know how much I didn't appreciate him being on my property. But in his scamper to get away, he ran right into Nick Flowers. He hit his head good and they took him inside. That's when—what's the guys name in the picture?"

"David. His name is David Alan."

"Your brother?"

"Yes, my brother."

"Well, your brother pulled out some sort of fancy camera and showed us footage of what he said was of the White River Monster." Rick shook his head. "I remember leaving there with my wife, telling him Photoshop can do amazing things. I'm not fooled by that nonsense."

"And then you never saw him again?"

"No, never."

"Are you sure?"

Rick sneered. "What do you mean am I sure? Of course I'm sure."

"No offense meant. It's just that the Flowers said they only saw him passing by. They never mentioned him having been in the house or the footage."

"Those two are a bunch of liars, and they are up to no good," Rick said. "I can't figure out what it is they do, and maybe I don't want to know." Rick turned on his heels and started to walk away but not before he gave Taegan his picture back. "Good luck getting the truth out of them."

Rick went inside his home. Taegan watched him, perplexed by his behavior. Then there was this dilemma with the Flowers. Why would they lie to him? They seemed so nice and normal. Maybe this Rick Hisster was a troublemaker.

Taegan traveled upstream and contemplated knocking on the Flowers' door to confront them. As luck would have it, Nick Flowers stood on the shoreline with a fishing pole and a bucket next to him.

"Hello, Taegan," Nick said. "Did you have any luck?"

"No. Nothing at all. Maybe I found what quiet can be like, but nothing more."

"How did you like it?"

"It's not for me," Taegan said and shivered. He stuffed his hands in his pockets.

Nick reeled in his line and placed his pole down. "You need to come in and warm up."

"Thank you," Taegan said. Nick played right into his plan.

"I'll have Marsha make you some tea or coffee," Nick said. "Which do you prefer?"

"I'll take some coffee. I can use the caffeine."

"Coffee it is," Nick said, and he entered his house. "How do you like it?"

"Black."

12

SURPRISE DRINK

Taegan was seated at the table. He looked around the small cabin. Simple kitchen, dining room, a closed door at the end of a hallway he figured was the master bedroom. There was another hallway, which he knew led to the guest bedroom he'd slept in, and there was a bathroom there, too. Everything was in its place, and there was a certain feeling of home while he sat and waited for his coffee.

"Here you go, Taegan," Marsha said and placed a stainless steel cup with a moose embossed into the side right in front of him. He stared at the cup for a moment, then looked at Mrs. Flowers. "Thank you so much."

"You're welcome. Just be careful. It's really hot."

Taegan nodded and looked at the cup again. There was no doubt that this was the cup his brother ordered off of Amazon. He needed to keep his composure and not let on to what he suspected.

Taking a few sips from the cup, he leaned back in his seat. "Mmm," he said. "Very good, but too hot to drink yet."

"We don't know who cleared that spot down river," Nick said. "But it's a popular location for people to go when searching for Whitey."

"That's the second time I heard that expression," Taegan said.

"What expression?"

"Whitey."

"That's what the locals refer to it as. We prefer that over calling it a monster."

"I see," Taegan said and took another sip of coffee. It had cooled down enough to drink. He sipped some more and made sounds of pleasure. He wanted to leave but also didn't want to seem nervous.

"Maybe one of these days someone will come away with some evidence and put this craziness behind us."

"I don't think it exists," Taegan said.

"Really?"

Taegan nodded. "Legends are just stories twisted and contorted over a period of time to confuse people. Secrets. That's what creates the allure. The unexplainable appeals to people."

Nick bobbed his head. "I never thought of it that way. That is really a compelling argument."

Taegan finished his coffee.

"One that I may use," Nick said.

"Please, by all means," Taegan said and stood. "May I use the restroom before I go?"

"Of course, you know where it is."

"Thank you."

Taegan went into the bathroom, shut the door, and tried to calm his beating heart and steady his hands, which he felt starting to tremble. He needed to control his anxiety because Nick had a watchful eye.

Five minutes later he came out with his emotions in check.

"I want to thank you both so much for your hospitality, but as you know, I must be going. I have a flight to catch, and I don't want to miss it."

"You're welcome. It was very nice meeting you, and I'm glad we were able to help. Can we offer you a ride into town? We have to go there anyway."

"No thank you," Taegan said. "This will be my last chance to enjoy nature before returning to the concrete jungle."

Taegan shook Nick's hand and gave Marsha a hug.

13

CAMOUFLAGE

Taegan left the house and immediately searched for the best place to hide. He needed thick cover but from a vantage point where he could watch the Flowers' every move.

Off to the left of the house was a tangle of bushes. He crawled into the foliage and faced the house, hoping he didn't give into the cold and make so much as a sound. He couldn't believe they served him coffee in his brother's cup. Were they somehow testing him to see what he knew? Maybe they were waiting for a reaction.

They were ballsy, and just like Rick Hisster said, they were up to no good—and he was going to find out what it was. His brother's life may very well depend on that.

Within an hour, he watched the Flowers get into their vehicle, ride up the driveway, and turn on the dirt road. He army crawled out of the thicket, stood, and ran to the house. He crashed his shoulder into the front door, and the frame splintered and gave way.

Like a bloodhound fresh on the trail, he ran into the master bedroom and went straight for the closet. That could be the only place.

When he turned on the light and opened the door, he stood there, shocked to see the closet packed with camping gear all the way up to the ceiling and almost spilling out the door. The last pack in was a bright red pack he suspected was his brother's. He dragged it out and opened it where he stood.

Piece by piece, Taegan withdrew from the pack the things he'd seen on David's Amazon order summary. There was a tent, pot, smashed camera, fire starters, and even some clothes he recognized as being his brother's. He dragged the pack out of the bedroom and placed it on the dining table. He strategically arranged each item on the table as if he were creating an exhibit. Then, after adding to the collection the stainless steel cup he found in the sink, he grabbed the largest knife out of the rack and sat at the table and waited.

He tried using his cell phone, but they were useless this far away from civilization. He had no plan but decided to hide the knife at his side. He waited. Hours went by, and he toyed with the cup. It was late in the afternoon before he heard the vehicle pull up. The rocks crunched underneath the tires and the engine shut down. There were no nerves, no regrets about what he'd done or hesitation about what he wanted to do. He turned askew and waited for them to come into the house.

Nick Flowers was first. He held a gun with a steady hand. Wide eyed and unsure, he looked right at Taegan and all the things splayed out on the table. Marsha was right behind him.

"What's this?" she said.

Taegan felt the knife at his side. "That's why I'm here. I need to understand what you're doing with my brother's pack."

"What are you doing in our house?" Nick said.

"Looking for my brother," Taegan said. "But I don't think I'm going to find him, am I?"

"You broke down our door!" Marsha screamed.

"Keep it down," Nick said. "He knows what he's done. What was it?"

Taegan moved the cup. "I searched his computer before I came looking for him. What's the likelihood that you would have the exact cup as him?"

"An oversight," Nick said.

"Yeah, a severe one."

Taegan went to stand.

"No, no, not a good idea." Nick waved the pistol as if to give direction with it. "Sit back down."

"He took the knife out of the rack," Marsha said. "He's hiding it near him somewhere."

"You can't come to a gun fight with a knife, son. Put it on the table."

"I knew before you gave me the cup, but I wasn't certain. Your kindness fooled me, made me doubt."

"Let me guess . . . Mr. Hisster has been sticking his nose where it doesn't belong?"

"You made an error, or I would never have known. You said you only saw him, not that he came into your house. The camera?" Taegan held it up and dropped it on the table. "He caught evidence, and you covered it up. Hisster thought it was a fake, but you knew it was authentic."

"We can't let that get out there."

"So you killed a man over it?"

"I didn't kill anyone."

"Marsha then?"

"No. Neither one of us killed. Now, I said to put the knife on the table."

Taegan reached for the knife and Nick stiffened. "Easy now. Nice and slow."

Taegan placed the knife on the table and Nick nodded at Marsha. "I'm a quick shot. Don't make me nervous."

"I'm not planning on it, and I don't doubt that."

Marsha came up behind Taegan with a belt cinched around each hand, pulled tight. She slung it over his head and brought it around his neck and squeezed. She pulled as hard as she could and the leather squeaked. Taegan was pulled onto the floor, and his weight took Marsha down with him. She pulled as hard as she could again, and Taegan tried to pull the belt away, but it was too tight. He felt extreme pressure in his head and face, and soon after, the blackness came over him.

14

WHITEY

The Flowers worked in tandem, not even having to use words to communicate what they had to do. Nick propped Taegan up against what Taegan— pretending to still be knocked out—assumed was the same tree they'd tied David to. Marsha worked the rope around his waist and chest, and Nick continued to struggle with the dead weight.

With one single chance and all of his might, Taegan threw a right haymaker that connected with Nick Flowers' face. A bone-crunching crack landed right on his chin and dropped him right where he stood. Before Marsha could react, he threw a second punch, this one with more behind it than the first. His awareness was coming back fully. She crumpled to the ground, and Taegan pulled himself free of the rope that Marsha was unable to tie off.

Taegan went to work and bound both Marsha and Nick to the tree, leaving them in a sitting position, making a knot he'd learned from his Boy Scout days—one that he remembered was impossible to get out of.

Unsure what was going on here, he retreated into the trees and hid. His neck hurt from the belt that had been cinched around his throat, but he forced down the need to cough, keeping himself quiet. He waited to see why they brought him here, back to the clearing.

He didn't have to wait too long. Splashing at the water's edge drew his attention and something slithered onto the land. The creature stood upright, and Taegan gauged the beast to be eight feet tall or better. It had gray shimmering skin; the face was very narrow and distinct. The eyes were small and hidden behind hundreds of tiny fins, but the mouth had an odd, beaklike shape. Gnarled teeth opened and snapped shut as it emerged from the shoreline and approached the Flowers.

Taegan moved carefully to try to get a better look at what was about to happen. He headed closer to the water and hoped the raging rapids covered any sound he produced. There, he found a tree to hide behind that allowed just his eyes to look around the trunk.

The creature bent, took Nick's face in webbed hands, and moved his head side to side. The beast gurgled. It then did the same thing to Marsha, and it stood. It looked around, and Taegan pulled himself behind the tree.

He waited and looked out from behind the tree. What he saw confused him more than the actual physical appearance of the White River Monster. It broke the rope with ease and freed the couple. With one more look around, the creature returned to the shoreline, got down on its belly, and slithered into the water.

Taegan needed to get out of there and fast. He turned to run but bounced off of something cold and wet. He fell to the ground and looked up and saw the monster towering over him. The thing had tentacles and fins but looked humanoid. The teeth protruded and were razor sharp. They gnashed together and made the most terrible sound. The smell that emanated off the beast was of the deep, and it was sickening.

Taegan backpedaled and tried grabbing for anything. His fingers wrapped around a club-shaped branch and the creature stepped forward. The pinhole eyes revealed nothing about the strange beast other than that it was animalistic and blood crazed. Taegan stood and swung for the face as hard as he could.

The branch crashed into its face and fell out of Taegan's hand. The monster howled as teeth broke away and flew through the air. Taegan turned to run, and the animal leapt and tackled Taegan to the ground and pinned him there, holding him still. The moisture from the fishlike body dripped in his face, and the weight that was on top of him was incredible.

Nick and Marsha Flowers stood over Taegan and looked down on him. They bore the wounds of his attack on them.

"You are the first to ever get the chance to fight back. You should be honored. I'm sure Whitey isn't happy and has something special in store for you."

Nick petted Whitey on his fishy human head and then held Marsha's hand and walked away. "You should've left while you had the chance instead of breaking into our house."

"Screw you! You fed my brother to this animal!"

"And now you," Nick said, his voice fading into the distance.

"Please don't leave me," Taegan screamed. His fear was palpable and his death certain. The only question that remained was how painful it was going to be.

Whitey grabbed his prey by the ankles with his webbed hands and dragged him to a nearby tree. He spread Taegan's legs and pulled him to the tree so that his crotch was on the trunk and each leg was on either side of the tree. The monster pulled, and Taegan's legs tore off at the hips. The creature dropped the limbs and flipped Taegan's body over and pressed his head against the trunk and pulled his arms on either side of the tree.

Taegan's neck broke from the force of the steady pull, and his arms broke away at the shoulders. Whitey removed the head from the trunk of the body with several twists and then gathered all the pieces and dragged them to the shoreline. He got down onto his belly and slithered into the water and disappeared into the wild, white-capped rapids.

15

GONE MISSING

Melinda Alan paced the berber carpeted floor, her focus deep within. She had gone back and forth from one end of the room to the other so many times, it was surprising there wasn't a hole worn right through the tightly looped material. Her fingernails had been chewed down so low her fingertips bled, but she didn't feel the pain.

She hadn't slept the entire night, spent the entire day going back and forth in her bedroom, and now a new night had settled upon her and her eyelids felt like bricks. She looked in the mirror and tried to talk herself into believing everything was going to be all right. But her words fell flat and were unbelievable. Her reflection even doubted her thoughts, and the feeling in the pit of her stomach that something was terribly wrong clung to her and wouldn't let go. The rings around her eyes were dark purple, and she had descended into a personal hell where every doubt and worry consumed her every thought.

She hadn't heard a word from her husband, Taegan, since he landed in Newport, Arkansas to search for his brother, David. David had gone missing a little more than a week ago.

Taegan found out where his brother went when he looked through the computer at David's apartment three days ago. Taegan had come home in hysterics and said he was going to look for him, that he was certain his brother was in trouble. She told him she didn't think it was a good idea that he went alone. She suggested he call the local authorities and let them look. But there was no stopping him. He packed a bag and was out the door in a hurry.

She couldn't help but think her husband had befallen the same fate as her brother-in-law, and it made her sick to her stomach. Worry consumed her and made her body shake and she couldn't eat. All she could do was continue to pace the floor and fall deep into indecision mixed with all the bad feelings she was experiencing. It came all at once and it repeated itself over and over again. What if she was overreacting and created a stir that brought Taegan all sorts of attention? He was a private man and he might walk in the door right after she made a call to the authorities.

But she could no longer handle the feelings of dread, doubt, fear, and anxiety. If Taegan came home, so be it. He could be upset, angry, or whatever. What she was about to do was for him, driven by the love she had for him. She picked up the phone and called the only person she could think of.

"Hey, Melinda," Ailish Becrux said.

"Hey, Ailish," Melinda said. "I'm sorry to be calling so late . . . it's just that . . ." she fell into silence or otherwise she would cry.

"What's wrong?"

"I've been pacing the floor for days, and I haven't been able to sleep or eat."

"What's going on? Why didn't you call me?"

She couldn't hold it back. Melinda started to cry hysterically and Ailish allowed her time. Soon Melinda regained control and tried to keep herself together so she could tell her what was going on.

"I'm sorry," she said, and needing her sister's compassion and toughness.

"Melinda?" Ailish said, the compassion there.

"OK," she said and breathed into the phone. "It's Taegan." Her voice was near a whisper, quivering.

"Taegan? What happened to Taegan?"

"He's gone missing, Lish. He went to look for David."

"Wait, he went looking for David where?

"David went missing over a week ago, and I told Taegan I didn't think he should go after him, but he wouldn't listen. He told me what he knew and then left. He doesn't know those people there or what he might be getting himself into."

"Let's not worry about that right now," Ailish said. "Just try and stay on track to what you remember."

"It all happened so fast I don't even know how much of it I retained. I went out after him, but he was already in his car and down the street. I haven't been able to get him on his phone, and I'm so afraid of what might have happened to him."

"OK," Ailish said. "I'm coming over right now. I want you to gather yourself and write down everything Taegan told you. You need to do that because it might help you remember. The smallest of details could mean all the difference."

"All right," Melinda said and nodded her head. "I can do that."

"Good. Give me fifteen minutes, and I'll be there. Have the door unlocked."

"OK."

Melinda unlocked the door and grabbed a pad and a pen and tried to steady her shaking hand enough to write the things she could remember. Everything was a blur.

16
FAMILY

"I need you to tell me everything you can remember," Ailish said. Melinda's sister had arrived in ten minutes, and everything about her was business. Here was the toughness.

Melinda looked at her notes. They were mostly illegible. "It has something to do with David going to Arkansas."

"Do you know what part?"

Melinda hesitated. "Umm . . . Newport, I think. No, I'm certain he said Newport."

"See? That's good." Her sister's soothing voice reminded Melinda of when they were young; the way her sister coached her. "Do you mind if we sit on the couch? I think we better do that."

"No, I don't mind at all. I can't remember the last time I sat. I've been pacing for days."

"Good, then this will be good to help calm you."

They went to the plush couch and sat. They sank deep into the cushions and were buried in pillows.

"Do you know why David went there? Did Taegan say anything about that?"

"Taegan said it had something to do with an Arkansas legend that originated out of Newport." She dabbed her eyes. "It's called a White River Monster or something stupid like that. He thinks he was looking to do a story on it and maybe he got tangled up with some bad locals or something."

"Newport, Arkansas is quite the trip for David to make to cover a story."

"Tell me about it. Especially since he was having a hard time making money, and I think he was

becoming desperate. Like it was all in or nothing."
She wiped her nose. "We tried to help him, but
David was too proud."

"This is all good information you're giving me."
Ailish wrote some things down. "We are going to
need to move quickly on this."

Melinda nodded. "OK, yes, of course. I wish we
could go now."

"I'm worried about you, Melinda," Ailish said.
"First, you need to rest. You look like you've been
through hell."

"I have been."

"I'm going to go to Newport and get this figured out."

"I need to go."

"No," Ailish said. "That's not a good idea."

Melinda raised bright red eyes to her sister. "I'm
going with you."

"No, you're not."

"What am I going to do? Sit around this house
and wait to hear from you? I can't do this anymore.
I need to go. I need to know what's going on."

"I understand your need to know. I'll keep in
touch."

"That's what Taegan said, and I haven't heard a
word from him. I can't do that again. I just can't."

Ailish fell into silence, looked at her sister, and
rubbed her face. She sighed. "If you were to come,
what would you do?"

"I'd like to help you. This may sound stupid, but
it can be like one of those adventures we used to do
when you were going through the academy. We'd set
up a scenario and we'd do it together."

"But this is for real, Melinda."

"You don't need to tell me that, Lish. My husband
is missing, and I'll do anything within my power to
help find him. You can't deprive me of that."

Ailish shook her head. "No. No, I shouldn't."

"Maybe there's a way you can use me to get to the boys. Whatever it is, I'd be willing to do it."

"All right," Ailish said. "It sounds like we're going to be taking a trip to Newport, Arkansas in the morning. I'm going to meet with the captain first thing and ask that he put me on the case. He owes me a ton of favors, and I believe this requires my attention. I know he'll give me the green light and make sure I have the full cooperation of the local law enforcement if I need it."

"How do you know?"

"That's how things work in the bureau sometimes," Ailish said. "Favors. Who you know. What you've done."

"Thank you," Melinda said.

Ailish rubbed Melinda's arm and gave her a warm smile.

"Let me go and see what you have in the fridge for us."

Ailish went into the kitchen, and Melinda could hear her rummaging through the refrigerator, the clink of glasses. Shortly, Ailish returned with a glass of blush wine for each of them.

"This should help calm you down and allow you to get some sleep. Come on, drink up."

Melinda's tremble was obvious as she drank the wine in long gulps. She had become desperate to escape the nervousness that coursed through her body and wouldn't leave her alone.

"I'll wake you before I leave in the morning. I'm going to stay the night—no arguments—and when I get up I'm going to headquarters first thing in the morning, and that'll give you time to get ready."

"I'm definitely going?"

"You are, and I don't want you alone tonight."

Melinda cried harder. There was nothing she needed more than a friend. With Ailish, she had that. Even though her sister was busy with her work in the FBI, she just dropped everything like that to help her out on a silly notion that something might have happened to her husband, and she used her favors to do so.

"Remember, when you get up, your job is to pack and be ready to go on a moment's notice."

Melinda nodded.

"If something is going on there, we will get to the bottom of it. I promise you that."

"I can't thank you enough, Lish. I've been so worried and wasn't sure if I should call you or not."

"You should have called earlier, but I don't want to upset you any more than you already are."

"I know I should have, but I didn't want to believe what I was thinking could be true. I was waiting for the phone to ring."

"Whenever you need me, Melinda, you call. That's what sisters do for each other." Ailish hugged Melinda. "Now, let's try to get some sleep. We're going to have a busy few days."

Ailish retrieved a blanket out of the hallway closet and a pillow off the bed. She laid it out and encouraged her sister to lie down. She took the wine glasses, shut off the light, and went to the computer on the other side of the house and started investigating what was known about this White River Monster.

17
CONTACT

The captain shared Ailish's concern about the missing men. After they ran credit card transactions from both men and verified they were indeed in Newport, the fact that their activity had suddenly stopped raised concern. It was low priority—probably not on the level of needing to get the FBI involved—but it was worth a look anyway.

"This is my brother-in-law," Ailish said. "My sister is a wreck, and I have to help her."

"I understand." The captain swiveled in his chair. "Jumping local like this might ruffle a few feathers. I can't see sending anyone else in with you. You're going to have to go at this alone, and I'm going to give you three days."

"Three days is plenty. I'll get in and get out."

"I'll get you what you need."

"I'm going to have my sister with me. She's better off coming than staying home. She brought up a good point that I can't ignore. She doesn't want to be home, pacing the floor, wondering what's happening."

The captain sighed. "She's under your care."

"Of course. Thank you so much, Captain."

"Consider us even."

Ailish smiled.

"I want you to be careful and report in when you're able."

"I can do that."

"What's the approach?"

"I'm not really sure yet. I'll have a little time to think things through on the flight over. What I can tell you is that I have a sense of what is going on there, and I could be in and out in a day."

"Take care of your sister," the captain said. "Get in, find out what happened to those men, and get out. We can send the dogs in afterward if we need to."

"I'm not going to let a trail go cold."

"Don't be reckless on this, Ailish. I can see there's a lot of emotion involved. When it comes to family, we can do some desperate things."

"I'll keep my head about me."

The captain looked at her long and hard. He broke his stare.

"I'll have a private jet take you into Newport, Arkansas. The plane will be waiting for you and your sister."

The captain, like Ailish, seemed as though he felt time was of the essence and didn't want them to lose time with layovers.

After a three hour flight, they arrived in Arkansas. When they disembarked from the plane, there was a black car waiting for them. Someone in a black, neatly pressed suit with a full length coat handed Ailish the keys and went into the plane.

Ailish got into the car and turned it on. The car started right up, and Ailish looked at Melinda. She was unsure if her sister was cold or just nervous.

"Are you feeling OK?"

Melinda nodded, but Ailish wasn't sure she believed her. "I need you to listen to what I'm going to tell you. I didn't say anything during the flight because I didn't want to give you time to think about it. I have an idea for how we can get to the bottom of this, and it is going to require me to use you for help."

"OK."

"In the trunk of this car is a change of clothes for you. There is also a hiking pack, which you will need to take with you. The bag you packed stays with me in this car."

"Are you doing what I think you're doing?"

"I want you to know I'm going to protect you at all costs. Do you trust me?"

"Of course I trust you, Lish. Why else would I call you, beg you to let me come along so I could help, and then make the trip all the way here? You're the best at what you do, and if anyone has a chance of finding Taegan and David, it's you."

Ailish got out of the car, opened the trunk, and removed a large red backpack. Inside it was a pair of gloves, pants, a hat, minor camping supplies—such as a pot, a skillet, and a Sterno—and some canned food. Also, there was a camera. She got back into the car and placed the pack down between them.

"I need you to change into this and play the part of a tourist . . . someone looking for the White River Monster."

Melinda nodded with obvious hesitation.

"Listen to me," Ailish said and turned askew in the driver's seat and fixed her sister with a firm stare. "There's something going on here for two grown men to check in and not check out. I need you to be the tourist, the bait, but I want you to understand you will never be alone."

"OK," Melinda said and started to change her clothes in the privacy of the car's tinted windows.

"If you follow my direction and give me that trust you say you have, we will be OK." Ailish grabbed Melinda's hand, and her sister paused in the act of changing. "We will be OK, and we will figure this out; find where the boys went."

Melinda squeezed her sister's hand and finished changing.

"I'll be driving this car, following you wherever you go," Ailish said. "You are going to hail a cab and find out how to get to the White River Monster. If we get there, we figure out where Taegan and David are. It is time for you to do some detective work."

"I'm a little bit nervous doing this."

"Just remember why you're doing this. Here, you are doing something, whereas at home all you were doing was waiting. This is your chance to help find your husband."

"OK." She nodded. "I can do this."

"Here," Ailish said. "I want you to put this on. It is a microphone and a tracking device. I'd prefer you place it on your shirt, under your coat, up high enough that I can hear you. Inside the camera is a recording device. It works like any other camera so no one will know the difference."

Melinda smiled. It seemed that the relief of knowing she could be found if things went south allowed a certain sense of comfort to come over her.

"I told you, we've got this."

"Yeah," Melinda said. "We've got this."

"One last thing I need you to do, and it is probably the most important thing." Ailish handed her a small, thin black square device no bigger than a quarter. "This is a wireless voice transmitter. I need you to drop it inside the vehicle that takes you to the White River. Can you remember to do that?"

Melinda nodded her head.

18

CONNECTIONS

Melinda looked down the busy road and saw her sister sitting in the running car. The puff of exhaust dissipated in the frigid wind.

"I hope you can hear me," Melinda said into the small microphone connected to her shirt. "I'm a little nervous right now."

One after the other, yellow cabs lined up, waiting for potential customers. Melinda approached a cab, pulled open the back door, and hauled her gear into the back seat with her. She wore North Face pants, jacket, gloves, and a hat that covered her ears. No one would question whether or not she knew what she was doing as she appeared ready to combat not only the weather but the terrain as well. She looked the part.

She had packed the camera in the backpack to make transporting things easier.

"Where might you be heading, young lady?"

Melinda put her nerves aside and remembered why she was there and why she was doing this. "I'm hoping to find the White River Monster."

The driver turned around in his seat and had a displeased look about him. He wasn't good at hiding his frustration. "Listen," he said, and his tone was as biting as the cold wind. "I can appreciate you reporters and enthusiasts coming here to Newport in search of this monster. You help our economy a little, but not enough that it's worth the aggravation. I don't know what your gig is, but I think you'd have a better chance of catching Big Foot than you do this White River Monster. I hear

Washington and California have had the most sightings of that big hairy ape. Go there. Focus on something you might have a real chance at catching a glimpse of. At least some evidence has been videotaped or photographed." The driver faced forward. "All these years, and nothing has been presented about our supposed monster. I'm sorry, I can't help you. Please, take your pack and go. I'd like to make some money tonight, but your ghost hunt is something I'm not interested in being a part of."

Melinda was stunned. A ride from one place to another still cost a fare that she was more than willing to pay. She wasn't going to debate that fact, so she grabbed her pack and exited the cab. The pack was much heavier than she would have liked it to be, but she knew it had to look authentic in case someone wanted to see what she was carrying.

Stepping to the next cab behind the one she exited, she knocked on the window. The driver rolled the window down and didn't say a word.

"I'm looking to go where the White River Monster might be located. Can you take me there?"

"I can't," the cabbie said. "But for a fee, I can take you to someone I know who can."

"What type of fee?"

"Because you're so nice looking, I'll cut you a break and do it for twice the fare."

Melinda had the money but needed to be smart about it.

"How do I know this person can get me where I need to go?"

The cabbie laughed. "Oh, he can get you there. He's taken hundreds of people there."

"What's in it for you?"

"Double fare, lady. You want a favor from me, you're going to have to pay for it. So you can either stand out there in the cold and find someone else to take you or you can get in the back seat and I'll get you to the right person. Most cabbies want nothing to do with people like you, so I'm not sure if you're going to get much luckier than meeting me."

"What do you mean they don't want to have anything to do with people like me?"

"Monster chasers. Dreamers. People who chase after nothing—they think they're a little crazy."

Melinda stood there for a second and acted like she was contemplating what she should do before she submitted and climbed into the back seat. She was glad to get the weight of the backpack off her shoulders and the wind off her face.

"I can make a living off of this legend alone," the cabbie said. "I don't understand why the other cabbies turn your kind away. Look at what you're looking to pay."

"So you get a lot of people coming through?"

"I don't get them all, but I heard there was about five this month. I suppose you're number six unless another came into town today."

"My lucky number," Melinda said.

"You'll need more than a lucky number."

"Oh yeah, why's that?"

"Because you're chasing something that does not exist, and yet you're willing to pay top dollar. There is no river monster, you do understand that, don't you?"

"You don't know that," Melinda said and looked out the window and saw the faceless people waiting to head to their destinations fading away. "Every day new species are discovered. I believe I have a chance at finding it if it exists. I'm good at what I do."

"And so am I, and the things you say aren't unique. Everyone who comes through looking for the monster says that. Now I have to make a call to make sure my contact is available."

The cab rode down the smooth road, and Melinda acted like she was captivated by the passing landscape.

"I have someone interested in seeing Whitey," the cabbie said into the phone. "Are you available to take her?"

The cabbie went silent, listening to what the person on the other end of the phone was saying.

"It's a pretty lady. She's the National Geographic kind out to photograph beautiful things. She's dressed like she's done this a million times before."

There was another pause in the conversation.

"OK, I'll bring her. I'm on my way right now."

He hung up his phone.

"You're in luck," the cabbie said. "He's willing to take you there."

"I appreciate that."

"You're going to have to negotiate his fee. I have nothing to do with that."

"I understand that."

The ride continued without further conversation. The cab driver turned down a few streets before pulling into an industrial area. Melinda shrank in the seat and looked out the back window to see if she could spot Ailish, but she couldn't. The pounding of her heart beat the inside of her chest. She felt unsafe and vulnerable being around these men she didn't know or trust.

The cab pulled next to another parked cab where a fat man leaned against the hood of his car.

"His name is Johnny," the cabbie said. He reached his hand back. "Sixty bucks, and I'm out of here. If there's anything else you want to know about Johnny, you'll have to talk to him."

Melinda paid him, grabbed her pack, and exited the vehicle. She looked at Johnny and he looked at her. He lips upturned into a smile.

"A survivalist," Johnny said.

"I guess you could say that." Melinda kicked at the dirt to show her Keen hiking boots.

"You'll put those to good use. Where you're looking to go will put your skills and equipment to the test."

"That's why I came." She smiled.

"Confident or foolish, I don't know. I can't understand why someone would want to wander a long treacherous pass along a river in search of something everyone talks an awful lot about but no one can seem to find." He shook his head. "It seems ridiculous to me, but whatever."

"It may sound ridiculous to you, but it sounds like an opportunity to me."

"It's going to cost you a hundred dollars," Johnny said.

"That's reasonable, if you tell me what direction to go in when we get there."

"I throw that in anyway. I don't want you getting lost."

Melinda got into the back seat and hoped the wire she was wearing was picking up every word. If it wasn't, she wouldn't last outdoors for more than an hour. She knew nothing about rural survival, and the cabbie was quite clear about the terrain she would encounter. Putting the weight of the backpack in the mix created a real danger.

The driver got into the cab. Melinda watched him squeeze behind the steering wheel and breathe heavily as he did so.

"Call me Johnny Phatz."

"I'm Melinda."

"Pretty name. No sense in waiting any longer, is there? Last chance to back out."

"That's all right. I'm OK."

"If you say so."

The cab rolled forward, and although Melinda's confidence wavered, she was becoming better at this. She reached into her coat pocket, pulled out the small listening device, and dropped it on the floor. She moved it under Johnny's seat with her foot.

19

THE DROP OFF

Melinda got out of the cab and hated the way the cold felt on her exposed skin when she first departed from the warmth. A thought came into her mind as she shouldered her pack and walked to the driver's side. If the path ahead was anything like the dirt road she just traveled, she had a challenge ahead of her.

She paid Johnny their agreed fee and he pointed her in the right direction.

"Down this path here is where you want to go."

Melinda looked down the steep drop off and wondered how she was going to navigate that.

"How far is the journey?"

"About five miles. Stick to the river's edge and watch your footing. The rocks are loose and pose a tripping hazard. You don't want to twist an ankle or something worse."

"Why can't you get me closer?"

"The road curves up ahead and takes us away from the river. This is the best spot and has been used for years. Our business is done here. Good luck to you."

Melinda approached the steep embankment, leaned back, and slid down. Once at the riverside, she looked at the fast-moving body of water with white caps. The sound it created was like a stadium full of people cheering.

"White River Monster, we're coming to get you," she said into the microphone. "It's beautiful down here, Lish. I'm going to start walking the path and see how long I can last. I'll rest along the way as needed."

It was weird talking into a microphone, and yet she found comfort in it, too. The idea that she didn't know whether or not she was being heard was the nerve-wracking part. To imagine she was here all alone was frightening.

20
BUSTED

When Melinda left to hail a cab, Ailish had immediately called the Newport Police Department and requested a marked police unit to escort her on her assignment. She asked for their two best officers. The time had come for her to introduce herself to them.

"Ailish Becrux," she said. "FBI."

A female officer stepped forward and shook Ailish's hand. "Officer Antoinette Ferrara."

A male officer stepped forward and offered his hand as well. "Officer Craig Hassett. We're happy to assist you in any way we can."

"I appreciate that," she said and briefed them on why she was there and what her plan was. She went over it a second time and made sure they understood.

When she was satisfied that the officers were briefed, she got into her car and began to follow Melinda's path, staying in radio communication with the patrol car with a powerful Motorola radio. Next to Melinda's safety, their cover was one of the most important things they needed to maintain in order for this to work.

Ailish listened to Melinda's conversations intently. She was thrilled at how easy it was to make contact with the person who ushered people to the White River Monster, and she was impressed with how well Melinda was handling herself.

She heard her sister and the cab driver named Johnny part ways and even heard the grinding of the dirt underneath Melinda's boots as she slid

71

down the embankment Johnny instructed her to go down. Ailish changed the channel on her radio and listened to Johnny.

"Yeah, it's Johnny," he said, and Ailish knew he was speaking into a phone. "I just dropped off someone else. A female. She seems the survivalist type, so if she walks straight through she may be there sooner than most."

Silence.

"You can pay me next drop off," Johnny said, and she heard the beep of the phone being hung up.

Ailish moved in fast. She pulled in behind the cab, got out of her vehicle with her gun drawn, and approached the driver's side.

"FBI," she said. "Turn off the vehicle and put the keys on the dashboard."

Johnny shut off the car and placed the keys on the dashboard.

"I'm going to need you to step out of the car."

The marked patrol car pulled in behind Ailish's, and the officers assisted her in getting Johnny out of the car. They needed two sets of cuffs to bind his arms behind his back.

"Who did you call on the phone?" Ailish asked.

Johnny hung his head. "Damn."

"Your cooperation can only help you at this point."

Johnny shook his head.

"Officer Hassett, please get the cell phone out of the cab."

Officer Hassett did and held it up for Ailish to see.

"I want you to run the number of the last phone call he made. We need to know who that person is. Make sure we get an answer quick."

Officer Hassett walked to the patrol car and radioed it in. Within a minute he walked back to

Agent Becrux. "It is a phone number for a Mr. Nick Flowers. He lives on the riverbank approximately five miles upriver."

"I'd like you to take Johnny here to the precinct and detain him for aiding in kidnapping. Keep him until I return to the precinct."

The officers took Johnny to the car and squeezed him into the back seat.

"I want to thank you both for your help. I've got it from here."

The officers exchanged pleasantries with Ailish and drove away. Ailish slid down the slope and imagined Melinda had only a mile on her, two at the most. She followed the river, confident this was where both Taegan and David went.

Everything was going exactly as she planned.

21

THE REAL MONSTERS

Melinda came upon a break in the trees that had been to her right during the entire journey downriver. An old man with a pleasant face was gathering wood when he noticed her.

"Hello, young lady."

"Hello," she said. Tired from her journey, Melinda's back had an ache in it that could bring a large man to his knees.

"You look like you can use a rest. My wife is inside, and I believe she has some gumbo soup made," the old man said.

That sounded so good to Melinda she almost groaned. "I thank you for the offer. I would love to come in and relax. Lord knows I could use a warm meal in my belly."

"The journey upriver is tougher than most people think. Take your pack off, and I'll carry it inside for you."

Melinda was all too eager to take the man up on his offer. She knew it wasn't quite that much, but it felt like a hundred pounds was lifted off her shoulders.

"I'm Melinda Degraff," she lied, using her maiden name. She was unsure who she was in contact with and if this man or his wife knew anything about Taegan or David. If they had come across them and had given their last name, she could be putting herself in danger—provided something dangerous had actually happened to them. Although the man seemed easy enough to trust, she couldn't be certain of anything.

"I'm Nick Flowers, and my wife is Marsha Flowers. She's such a gentle soul. You'll love her."

"I'm sure I will. I can't tell you how nice it is to meet you," Melinda said.

"Come on in. Let's get you seated in front of the fireplace and give you a nice big bowl of warm soup to eat."

"Thank you," Melinda said. "This is a beautiful cabin."

"And I thank you," Nick Flowers said. "It is only one of two cabins built this close to the river on this side. We love the solitude."

They entered the cabin, and Melinda seated herself near the fire upon Nick's suggestion.

"Marsha, this is Melinda," Nick said. "She was traveling the path and I just so happened to run into her. I offered for her to sit in front of the fire and even told her you might give her a bowl of that wonderful gumbo soup you made."

"I would love to. It's still hot." Marsha went to the kitchen.

"Would you like to make yourself comfortable and take off your coat? If you start to sweat underneath it and then continue on your journey, you might be in danger of hypothermia."

"No, but thank you," Melinda said. "I'm quite comfortable, and I don't think I'll be staying too long. I know I have about three hours of daylight left, and I'd like to get farther upriver."

"I suppose you're here for the White River Monster?"

"I am," Melinda said. "I've read so much about him or her that I had to come and see for myself."

"I can tell you where you need to go."

"Any help you could give me would be greatly appreciated."

"Continue on the path you're on, and not too far from here is a circular cutout. That's where people claim to have the most sightings of Whitey."

Marsha set the bowl down in front of Melinda. She ate like she hadn't eaten in a week.

"I think she likes it," Nick Flowers said.

Marsha smiled. "It is my pleasure when I can provide someone with comfort."

A bead of sweat formed on Melinda's brow and ran down her face.

"You're going to need to take that heavy jacket off," Nick said. "I guarantee that shirt underneath is soaking wet now."

"No worries. It's Under Armour. It helps keep the sweat away from my body."

"Still, it's not good to be sweating the way you are and then looking to step out into the cold."

"I'm OK," Melinda said. "Really, but thank you."

Nick looked at Marsha and Marsha locked eyes with her husband. This didn't escape Melinda's notice, and she knew she needed to get out of there.

"I should be going. Thank you for your hospitality. I'm going to grab my pack and head out."

"No," Nick said and rested a hand on her shoulder. "You're my guest, and I need to make sure you leave here safe and prepared for the last leg of your journey."

"I'll be fine."

"Take off your coat and give the fire a chance to dry out your layers underneath. You won't lose much time, and you'll be much safer for it."

"That's not necessary."

"Oh, but it is."

Nick Flowers reached for the zipper and Melinda latched her hand onto his. "What are you doing?"

"Helping you."

"Get your hands off of me."

Nick looked at his wife, and Melinda turned her head just in time to see what she thought was a rolling pin slam across her head. She saw stars, became dizzy and disoriented. She wanted to protest, but everything was going in and out of focus.

"Hit her again," Nick Flowers said.

Marsha didn't hesitate. This time, putting her hips into the swing, she smashed Melinda on the back of the head, and she fell limply out of the chair.

"She's hiding something," Nick said.

"I know it," Marsha said. "I sensed it too when you asked her to take off her coat."

"Help me get the coat off of her."

They stripped the coat off of her and immediately found the wire clipped to her shirt underneath. The couple looked at each other with concern.

"Why do you suppose she is wearing that?"

"I don't know, but let me call Johnny and see if he's all right."

Nick dialed Johnny, and the phone rang three times before he picked up. "Yeah?"

"Is everything OK?"

"I'm on a run. Why, is everything OK with you?"

"The woman you dropped off was wearing a wire."

"A wire? What kind of wire?"

"One clipped to her shirt, I don't know."

"Hmm, maybe she's recording every aspect of her trip? That's popular with these outdoorsy people."

"Do you know how these things work?"

"It's just like a microphone and records to a device. It's that simple."

"What kind of device?"

"A cell phone, iPad . . . anything bluetooth, I suppose."

"Well, we have her unconscious and she's bleeding pretty bad. Marsha gave her two good smacks to the back of the head. We can't let her go now."

"Understood. It's a shame, really. She was a real pretty woman."

"Yes," Nick said. "'Was' being the key word."

Nick Flowers hung up the phone.

"I think Johnny is right. We can spend hours looking for this recording device or just get her set up by the cutout and send her things down the river."

"What about the Hissters?"

"Those two . . . they're a pain in the ass and have often come too close to getting in our way. We may have to deal with them soon. They're on vacation and they won't be back for another two days, so we'll leave that for another day."

"OK," Marsha said. "Let's get this over with."

22
KIDNAPPED

Ailish was moving quickly now, worried about the danger Melinda was in. She used brilliant strategy sending her in with a wire, but the Flowers were on to her.

Ailish pulled out a phone with satellite capabilities and called the precinct. "I'm heading to the Flowers residence. They caught on to what they think is Melinda's motivation and they knocked her out. Send a car to their house."

"Right on it," the voice boomed through the phone. "The Flowers called here, and we put Johnny on the phone to try and throw them off."

"That was a brilliant move. You people know exactly what you're doing."

"Thank you."

"I've got to hang up and get to Melinda."

Ailish hung up the phone and navigated the rough terrain as fast as she could. About fifteen minutes later, she came upon the Flowers' cabin and saw that their vehicle was still there. She drew her weapon, looked in through some windows, and breached the front door. She went room by room, using her weapon as her lead, but found no sign of the couple or Melinda. Pieces of thick rope were discarded next to a massive blood stain on the floor next to the table.

Over and over again through the radio chatter she had heard about this cutout a little farther up the river. With no time to call and wait for backup, she ran out the door and headed upriver, unsure exactly how far she needed to go.

She heard shuffling up ahead and slowed her approach and tried to remain as quiet as she could. She was unsure if the people she was after had weapons or not, and they knew the lay of the land much better than she did, giving them an advantage. The element of surprise was the only thing she had on her side.

"Hang in there, Melinda, I'm coming to get you out of there," Ailish said, gripping her weapon dependently.

23

WAITING FOR THE RIGHT TIME

Ailish finally made it to the circular cutout she'd heard everyone talking about. Night had started to fall, but she could see Melinda and the couple well enough. They were tying her to a tree, working in tandem with few words spoken between them. Ailish knew this meant they had done this before—probably many times.

Melinda's shirt was blood soaked and she was unconscious. Ailish reached for her phone, but it was gone. She must have lost it in her mad dash to catch up to her sister.

Everything inside Ailish made her want to shoot the Flowers and take them down quickly, but she didn't trust the angle and didn't know what sort of weapons they had. As difficult as it was, she needed to allow things to play out until the advantage turned to her favor. She needed to be smart. That would keep her sister alive, she was sure of it.

They finished tying Melinda, and her head flopped forward; the gash on her head actively dripped blood. Drawing a deep breath, Nick Flowers slathered his hands in Melinda's blood and went to the river's edge. He washed his hands in the water and then dried his hands on his pants.

"That should be enough for him to smell."

"Yes," Marsha agreed. "He should be here soon."

"Do we stay and watch?"

"If you'd like," Marsha said. "It has been awhile."

"Yes, it has."

About a minute passed before Ailish heard noise off to her left. In the circular opening, a beast slid out of the water on its belly and stood. The thing was giant. Eight feet tall or better, it had brown skin and fishlike features but also resembled a human. Webbed hands, bulging needlepoint teeth, and unforgettable eyes that were mere dots devoid of compassion were easy to see even in this fading light.

A chill rocked Ailish's body, and it wasn't from the cold. She listened to the thing gurgle as it breathed. It looked at the elderly couple, and they smiled at the beast as if they adored it.

It walked to Melinda and took her head in its hands and moved it side to side. It was appraising her, Ailish realized, but she felt like it was appraising her, too. The tongue came out of its mouth and it tasted her sister's blood.

Something about that moment made Ailish snap. She couldn't take what she saw anymore and rushed out from her cover, aimed her weapon at the monster, and took a shot. The bullet penetrated the right shoulder and it howled out in pain. It grabbed its arm and growled at Ailish something inhuman.

She sensed the Flowers running toward her, and they were easy targets.

Pop. Pop.

Both shots landed dead center in each chest. They fell, and she turned to empty the clip into the monster when she watched it grab Melinda's head and pull it. Yanked from her shoulders, her sister's head and a portion of her spine dangled from the creature's grasp. Ailish screamed out and unloaded her weapon into the giant monster. It staggered backward, fell to a knee—but then it stood. It moved forward, blood dripping from the holes that punctured its skin.

Behind Ailish, a second monster slithered ashore and stood up and charged her. It knocked down thin trees with ease, and it reached her as she aimed her weapon and heard the dull click of an empty clip.

The monster hit her with a stiff arm. Devoid of breath, all she could do was watch the monster drag her by her feet. The hard, rough ground hurt her back. Broken tree limbs slashed her skin, and if she could have she would have yelled out in pain. She watched the monster she shot dismantle her sister, breaking away body parts piece by piece in a frenzied fit.

The monster that dragged Ailish stopped at a tree, kept her prone, pressed her back against the tree, and put its cold, awful-smelling hand underneath her chin and pulled on her ankles and head. Her spine cracked and bent around the tree. Her suffering was short.

The monsters looked at the Flowers' dead bodies and howled. Other monsters surfaced in the water and looked ashore.

The monster Ailish shot grabbed the Flowers' bodies and took them to the shore. He petted their heads, placed his ear hole to their chests, and then to their mouths, and listened.

The monster got up and made some gurgling sounds directed at the other monsters that remained offshore. They were quick to come and grab the Flowers' bodies and pull them into the deep. The two monsters that remained on land took Ailish to the shore and stacked Melinda's body parts on the shoreline.

The monster Ailish shot went back to the tree, cut the rope away, and used it to tie the body parts together. He took it into the water with him, and the other grabbed Ailish's body and dragged it into the water.

Together, the monsters swam away, hidden by the white caps, swimming upstream to a den where the family would eat well this night.

24

DANIEL

Daniel Happ walked through the thick forest just beyond the White River. The sound of the rushing rapids was a constant background noise, and to Daniel, it mimicked the breeze hurrying through the trees above.

A dead raccoon dangled from his hand by its tail. The body had gone stiff from lying in the trap overnight. Baited with a frog, the coon was an easy catch, really. Daniel had set the Paiute deadfall trap just before it was time to go home, and he'd thought about it all night, excited to find what he would catch the next day.

After he roamed the forest a bit trying to locate where he put the trap, he found himself turned around. He happened to hop a log, and that's when he saw the hind end of the animal hanging out of the trap.

He pumped his fist and slid away the rock that had crushed the animal's head. Each little victory meant the world to him—especially since he was able to do it himself.

Some years back, he had located a semicircular cutout in the woods that was both private and perfect for him to do the things he loved. He was often kept away by campers and made it his business to keep away from them. He didn't know them, and his mother told him not to trust anyone. She was honest about his being slow and what that meant, but Daniel really didn't understand. So he did what he loved to do. He roamed the forest and visited the river looking for things to do.

Now, he approached the cutout to see if anyone was there, and he found the area empty. The river, the cutout, and the thoughts that wanted to come out of his mouth were the only things around him.

He didn't like it when the outsiders came. Sometimes he found himself watching them from a distance to see what they were doing. Most of the time they weren't doing anything, but other times he had witnessed some strange things he was unable to understand. He tried not to think about the fear he sometimes felt when he saw those things.

While the campers were there, he had plenty of woods to wander and could attempt to catch his prey and explore. He made it his business to remain hidden and far enough away to avoid detection and instead focused on what he loved to do: hunt, trap, and kill.

Daniel straddled a large boulder just beyond the cutout, removed his eight-inch Buck knife from its sheath, and slapped the animal onto the rock. He positioned the animal so that he could gut it. He would have to act quickly because he had spent an awful lot of time trying to find his trap. The sun would be setting soon, and that meant it was time for him to head home.

His house was up the hill, across the road, and set back in a break in the trees. Whenever he was late, his mother would scold him and ask him not to scare her, and he didn't like disappointing his mother or scaring her. She was all he had.

25
FAMILY

Hugh Greyson had opened the rental shack for the third day of the season, and not one single tourist had come through. Not one! Dusk was coming, and he would soon have to close. If his luck didn't change soon, things might get ugly in a hurry.

He was certain the disappearance of six people four months ago being smeared all over the news had played a big part in keeping people away. It was a good thing there were a lot of natural resources for a human being to live off of, though that didn't ease his concerns one bit.

Staying inside the cool shack, he sat and read Tom Sawyer for at least the fiftieth time. The fading light made it hard to see, but he could practically recite the entire book without having to see anything at all. Tom Sawyer was a classic, Mark Twain at his best, and like a favorite song, it never got old or boring for Hugh. To him, it was like the story had been written just for him.

The crunch of gravel stole his attention, and he looked out of his rental stand. If his eyes weren't deceiving him, he was watching a Subaru Outback with a California license plate pull up. The family of four poured out of the crossover SUV and ran for the stand. The brochure they had picked up at one of the motels along the highway was folded in the father's hand. The kids, in their early teens, Hugh guessed, couldn't contain their excitement.

"This is it," one of the teens shouted. "White River Raft Rentals! Crooked sign and all!" The teen pointed.

Hugh scowled. It was put that way on purpose.

"How are you doing?" the California man said to Hugh. "I'm George Rice, and this is my wife, Tammy, and my two sons, Chris and Eric."

"I'm doing just great," Hugh said and offered George his hand. "How are you?"

George turned and looked at Chris and Eric. "Well, how are we?"

"Ready!" Eric said.

"We so got this," Chris said. Tammy remained quiet; beautiful and shy.

"I think we're ready for a whitewater adventure!" George said. "I know it'll be getting dark soon though. Are you still open?"

"You'd be my last customer of the day."

Chris and Eric hopped around and Tammy watched on, quiet in her repose, as she had moved off to the side. She shook her head and made no attempt to hide her smile.

"Have you ever been white river rafting before?" Hugh said, leading the family around the back of the shack. He spoke loudly because the noise of the rapids required it.

"Everywhere we go and any chance we can get!" George said.

"Perfect," Hugh said and went to the rusted cage and pulled out a raft. He had checked the pressure first thing this morning as he always did, and he grabbed the paddles, vests, and, helmets. He passed them around.

The family started to dress in the necessary equipment.

"Remember, all protective gear is required to stay on at all times."

"I understand," George said. "Did you hear the man, boys?"

"Yeah," they said in unison.

"You'll love the water," Hugh said. "It's cool, but with the way that hot sun heated up the day like it did today, I think you'll find it refreshing. The sky is something to take in, too."

George looked out into the rapids and up into the pink, yellow, and blue sky. "Sure looks that way."

"Oh, cash only," Hugh said. "Machines went down earlier today, and it has been a battle to get someone out here to fix it. I'm sorry, I should have mentioned that before we pulled all this stuff out and got you dressed."

"No problem," George said. "How much?"

"Did you want a guide to go with you today?"

"No, that won't be necessary."

"OK. Then let's just say sixty and call it even."

George took three twenty dollar bills out of his wallet and handed them to Hugh.

"Thank you," Hugh said and pocketed the money. "You guys are going to launch right here." Hugh pointed at the smooth ramp of dirt and then downstream. "Once you step into the raft and the water pulls you into its current, hang tight. Some parts get real choppy, especially in the beginning."

George nodded.

"Now, about five miles downstream where the river bends, the whitecaps will simply disappear, and that is when you start to look right. There is a shack there, identical to this one, and there will be another man there by the name of Bill. He'll be expecting you. He'll get you guys pulled in, get the gear back from you, and drive you back here where you can pick up your vehicle."

"That sounds perfect," George said. He turned to his kids. "Are you guys ready or what?"

"We're ready! We're ready!"

"Do you have anything you need me to go over before I set you off?"

"No," George said. "I'd like to consider myself and my family to be seasoned pros."

"That's perfect," Hugh said. "The river may challenge those skills. You can leave your valuables here so they don't get wet."

He held out a plastic container with a lock on it. The father placed the car keys, his wallet, and his phone into the bin, and the rest of the family did the same with their personal belongings. Hugh locked the bin and gave the keys to George, who zipped them into a pocket on his vest.

"Sign here," Hugh said and held out a clipboard.

George didn't even read it before signing his name.

"I'll see you when you get back," Hugh said and held the clipboard at his side. "Enjoy your trip down the White River!"

Hugh watched the family climb into the raft and launch. The river whisked them away, and he watched them bounce down the rapids and shout their joy for the adventures of the great outdoors. He reached into his pocket and pulled out a Motorola radio.

"This is Hugh."

"Go ahead, Hugh."

"We got a family of four heading down," Hugh said. "Experienced and moving fast."

"Perfect," the voice on the other end clicked through. "Did you dump?"

"Not yet."

"Do it now!"

"Don't worry about me. You do your part."

Hugh went to the back end of the cage to a trashcan that had a strapped down lid. He opened it, moved his head away from the awful stink that smashed him in the nose, and removed a five gallon pail filled about halfway. He walked it to the river's edge and dumped it in. He watched the fast-moving water take away the rancid blood and guts, and then he rinsed out the pail and left it out.

He closed the shack, took the plastic container, and removed the car keys through a dummy side wall. He got into the car and drove away.

26

CAPTAIN

Marty Mallow sat at the table and contemplated the changes his life had taken in the past four months. A product of his own doing, he had left the FBI because he had sent his best agent into the field alone, thinking the assignment wouldn't turn anything up. Instead, he'd sent her straight into the arms of death.

Ever since that day, he'd been haunted by the question of how someone could live with something like that. The answer that came back was simple: with regret.

How could he have been so casual, had such oversight and not followed protocol? That answer, too, was also simple to find. He had become careless. Complacent.

Marty stood and tried to shrug the negative thoughts off as he walked from room to room of the quaint cabin that had belonged to Nick and Marsha Flowers. They were another couple that had gone missing around the same time that Ailish and her sister, Melinda, had disappeared.

The blood traces that could be positively identified belonged to David, Taegan, and Melinda. They'd found the traces in this house and in the same areas: in the dining area on the floor and on the walls and ceiling. Obvious clean up attempts had been made with bleach and other household products, but when the lights went out and the black light was turned on, it looked like a massacre. And yet there were no gouges in the wood anywhere, nothing to prove any signs of a struggle.

Marty had his theory, but without bodies it would remain just a theory. So he decided to move to Newport, Arkansas and purchase the sitting property with a promise to himself that he would dedicate the rest of his days to trying to find out what happened to his agent and her family.

Certain things made sense and others didn't. Ailish was smart, independent, and seasoned. He had a hard time accepting that there was no evidence left behind as to where she might have gone or how she had gotten there. Marty just couldn't find anything solid to go on, and the not knowing was maddening.

The personal guilt had aged him ten years and cost him his marriage. He walked away from it all because what he felt inside was worse than a cancer. How could he live with what he had done and try to love someone when he knew he couldn't?

There was a truth out there somewhere—an incident that took place inside this house or somewhere beyond—and he refused to allow the case to fade away into obscurity. Six people's lives were gone in a flash, and their bodies up and disappeared in this area. Was there a killer on the loose, taking them away and burying them? Sending them downriver? If so, Marty hoped to gain his attention so that he might have the chance to face him down.

27

ROUGH WATERS

The Rice family navigated the rapids like they were pros. Going limp as they entered huge dips and hopping over the rough lifts, they all maintained their positions within the raft. George was in the front left and Tammy in the front right. Chris and Eric were always in the back and were used as the muscle to help steer the floating bullet.

"I think this might be it, boys and girl," George shouted over his shoulder. There was a blind turn coming up, and he remembered what Hugh had said. "I think we conquered another river," George added.

Chris and Eric exchanged a high five.

"There's nothing we can't beat," Tammy said and looked over her shoulder at the boys. Her voice was hard to hear over the splash of the rapids, but the message went through.

As they rounded the corner, a sudden change took over the boys' faces as their expressions twisted into something of absolute terror.

Had they been on a course to colliding with a large boulder? Was the water rougher here when they thought it was smoothing out? Tammy turned around and looked.

Standing in the spray and splash of the White River, a massive, fishlike monster stood up to its shoulders awaiting the arrival of the raft. The strong current had no effect on it. They could see that the massive maw was filled with razor-sharp teeth, and as they grew closer, the mouth opened in anticipation and acceptance.

"Paddle right!" George shouted, and they all followed his instruction. Sinking the paddles deep into the churning waters, they used every ounce of strength to try to steer clear of the implausible obstacle. The raft started to make a sharp turn, but it was too late.

The monster reached out with one webbed hand and grabbed the side of the raft and pulled it toward him. The Rice family started to scream, looking for a place to escape, but there was nowhere to go. The beast opened its jaws and snapped its chops, the teeth gnashing together.

The monster's clawed fingers easily punctured the raft, and it deflated and dropped everyone into the water. Paddles floated away, and the current started to scatter the family. The monster reached out and grabbed the people closest to him: Chris, George, then Eric. When he grabbed them, he pushed them beneath the surface and held them there with little effort.

With its pinhole eyes, the monster watched the woman float away, the rapids making her bob up and down, thrashing her about, allowing her no control as it took her away.

The monster lifted the three he managed to capture. All were dead and ready to be taken back to the den.

Tammy gasped for air as she was spit out into smoother waters.

"George!"

Splash.

"Chris, answer me!"

Splash.

"Eric! Oh God, please!"

Tammy tried to swim against the current, but her efforts were for naught as she realized: The river pulled you wherever it wanted you to go, not the other way around.

Grabbed underneath her armpits and pulled onto a small boat that was adrift and barely able to handle the river, Tammy looked into the swishing of the water, desperate to find her loved ones.

"My family," she said. "My family was just attacked by a fucking monster."

"Your head is bleeding, ma'am," the driver of the boat said. "Were you wearing your helmet?"

"Yeah . . . what the fuck?" She didn't care to look at him.

"I'm asking you because your head is bleeding and you do not have a helmet on."

It must have fallen off in the chaos, she realized vaguely.

"Do you know whether or not you hit your head on a rock or something?"

"I don't know what I hit my head on and I don't care! I saw this big fucking fish—no, it was a monster that looked like a fish and man—and it was big enough to grab our raft and pop it. The teeth were huge and the eyes were filled with aggression. That thing dumped us into the water and started to grab us."

"I'm sure they're OK," the boat driver said.

"How could you say that?"

"Sometimes the current spins people around a bit before it spits them out."

Tammy finally looked at the man. He was middle aged and had a look of intelligence about him. She couldn't understand why he wouldn't understand. "No, they are not OK! I saw a fucking creature standing in the water devouring my fucking family! Why aren't you listening to me?"

"I've heard every word you've said, ma'am. I don't like the way your head looks. Let me get you to the shore and get you looked at by someone."

Tammy dove back into the water. The man used a hook on a pole to grab her life jacket and drag her back to the boat. She kicked and screamed as he pulled her back on board.

"What the hell are you doing? I have to go and help my family!"

"You can't help them by going out there, OK?" the man said.

There was something in his tone that made her pause. Tammy looked at him, and the expression he wore was as serious as what she had just seen.

"I saw something out there, didn't I?"

The man nodded. "Yes, you did."

"What was it?"

"We call him Whitey."

"What the hell is Whitey?"

"He's some of exactly what you said and something a bit worse."

"There was a damn monster standing in the water like it was cemented to the ground. I couldn't imagine how strong it has to be to be able to fight the current like that."

"He's very strong."

Tammy just looked at the man. Trauma, confusion, and numbness from being submerged in the cold water left her trying to figure out what happened. Maybe she did hit her head on a rock and this was all just a dream. She laid her head back, and the dizziness found her and twirled her about.

The boat's engine came to life with an unsteady putt and brought them to the shoreline in a hurry. The man helped Tammy out, and she was clumsy every step of the way. The man held her upright.

"I'm OK."

He glanced at her and hesitantly chanced letting her go.

"Are you sure" he said, and his hands hovered.

She rubbed her head and looked into the water. Debris floated by. She turned again to look at the man and ask him a question when he lunged at her and grabbed her around the neck and squeezed until the blackness caved in on her.

Using the life vest to drag her along, the man pulled the woman through the rocky shoreline and then found a spot to let her body rest. Along the water's edge, the ripples gently slapped the left side of her body.

He disappeared into the woods, went around to the circular cutout, and saw Daniel gutting a raccoon. The man picked up a fallen branch and grabbed it with a firm grasp.

Daniel clearly didn't hear the man come up behind him, so he cleared his throat. Daniel had just turned to see who was there when the man brought down a heavy branch across the side of his face and knocked him off the boulder and to the ground.

The man returned to Tammy and dragged her by her vest. Putting her off to the side in the cutout, he dropped the branch next to her.

The man then went to Daniel and picked him up and also put him down somewhat off to the side of the clearing. A second person arrived and the man started to bark orders.

"Get the stick in her hand," he said. "Get the knife off of the boulder and put it next to Daniel and make sure the tent gets put up quickly. Don't forget to stuff the gear inside and make it look like it was being lived in."

"I won't," the person said and started the tasks.

"I've got to go. You have it from here."

"Yeah, I've got this."

28

MARTY MALLOW

Marty's phone rang, and he recognized the number right away. It was one of his men from the New York office. He knew his colleague wouldn't stop calling until he picked up the phone.

"Yeah?"

"Captain?"

"I'm not your captain anymore, Pokorny."

"How are you doing?"

"No better than yesterday or the day before."

Roger Pokorny breathed into the phone. "You should've come back when no evidence was found, Captain. Your being there isn't doing you any good. I don't understand why you stayed."

"They missed something. They had to."

"But you oversaw everything yourself every step of the way."

Marty slammed his fist against the wall. "Then I missed something. That makes me sloppy."

"It has been four months. What are you hoping to find?"

"What happened to my best agent and her entire family is what I'm hoping to find, Roger. Shit, I'd do the same thing if it was you. I also want to know what happened to the people that used to live in this house."

"I can come down—"

"No. I don't want anyone else in danger if there is something else at play here."

"That's precisely why you need someone there with you."

"I'm not having you."

"When you say there might be something else at play, are you talking about the legend or something else?"

"I don't know, Roger. That's the damn problem here . . . that I just don't know."

"The new captain said I could go if you needed me. I'd be willing. If I come and we don't find anything, then you come back here and leave that alone. Your wife needs you."

"Ah," Marty said, caught up in a whirlwind of emotions. "I wish it was that simple."

"Sometimes it is. But from where you're standing, you can't see what I'm seeing. This thing is killing you. It's eating you up from the inside out. That's why I'm trying to help you."

"Please, do me a favor and stay there," Marty said. "I like that things have gone quiet for the locals here. Maybe that'll bring some stuff up to the surface."

"OK. I'll stay put, but if I don't hear from you at least once a day, I'm coming for you."

"I understand and almost appreciate it," Marty said and hung up the phone. He went out the door and looked around his back yard and traveled the path with his thoughts on the idea that he had missed something along the way. There had to be a morsel somewhere. Maybe if he went back to that cutout it would be there, waiting for him. All he needed was a break.

One freaking break.

"I keep telling you that I don't care that you were in the FBI," Rick Hisster said. "You're on private property, and I'm getting tired of you thinking you can just step foot in my yard whenever you feel like it."

"Is that so?" Marty said and picked a spot on Rick Hisster's chin where he was going to plant his fist if the man came near him.

"That is so."

Rick was like a dog that ran around his yard every day and marked the four corners of his turf. The tree he was figuratively chained to only left him enough room to reach those corners, where he sat in wait for someone to come onto his property so he could growl and bark.

"Let me ask you something, Rick," Marty said.

"Ask away. But you can do that by backing up a few steps and getting off of my property."

"No, I'm fine where I am," Marty said and looked where he was standing. Clearly he was on Rick's property. "Why are you so concerned about who walks on the back end of your property that you don't even occupy, when six people went missing four months ago?"

"Because I pay for that spot you're standing on." Rick smiled. "Now that I have answered your question, I have a question for you."

Marty nodded.

"Why do you live in the house of two people that disappeared during the same time your agent disappeared?"

"I'm hoping to find clues as to their whereabouts."

"Oh," Rick said and looked away. "And what have you found? Nothing, I presume, because they cleaned up after themselves."

Marty laughed. Rick didn't know about the blood spatter.

"No disrespect meant, but did you find anything else to help you locate your missing colleague or her family?"

Marty's hands curled into tight fists and his smile disappeared.

"I told you those people that lived in that house were no good when I first met you. They were secretive and manipulative, and yet you still moved in there for some odd reason. You think I'm weird?" He shook his head. "Walls don't talk, so I don't know why you're even there." He paused and stared at Marty. "Or why you're even here for that matter."

"You know exactly why. I want to know who killed my colleagues."

"Look at this area you're in," Rick said. "Maybe there's a crazed serial killer running around here and he got those people. Maybe he's moved on . . . I don't know. I think whatever you're doing is just wasting your time, and it's bothering me. I hate to say this, but I can see the guilt in your eyes, and I know that motivates you. It's not healthy."

Marty looked away. "I wish you'd come over here and say that."

"Well, it seems I got to you," Rick said. "You seem uptight."

Just then, the sound of tires crunching gravel drew both men's attention to a police cruiser coming up Rick's driveway. Officer Craig Hassett parked his vehicle and walked between the two men.

"How are we doing today, gentleman?"

"Couldn't be better," Rick said.

Marty looked in the direction of the opening.

"I was heading there myself," Officer Hassett said. "Would you like to come along?"

Marty nodded. "I was going anyways."

"Across my property," Rick said. "You know I don't want people using my yard as a thoroughfare."

"No one gives a shit about your yard or what you want," Officer Hassett said, and Rick crumbled visibly. "If you want to stop being a dick and come and join us, you're more than welcome. We could use the extra set of eyes."

Rick hesitated but soon fell in line with the men, and they walked toward the opening.

29

SETTING THE SCENE

Both Tammy and Daniel remained unconscious and off to the side as the second person continued to complete the tasks as instructed.

On the clearing near the White River, a tent was erected, and a backpack filled with necessities was tossed inside. An opened sleeping bag was positioned perfectly, and a pillow was placed at the back end of the tent. A campfire was lit in an existing circle of rocks intended for that purpose, and the smell of smoke filled the coming night air.

Moving onto the woman, the life vest was removed and the stick that was dropped beside her was placed into her hand. The Buck knife that belonged to Daniel was placed on his abdomen.

The raccoon that was on the rock was left where it was, and the person went over to Tammy. The person snapped an ammonia capsule underneath Tammy's nose and then quickly did the same for Daniel. The two started to rouse, and the mysterious person disappeared into the thicket and hurried away with the life jacket.

30

RURAL

Hugh drove the Rice family's vehicle for an hour before he finally turned off into the thicket. Weaving the vehicle among the trees, he scratched and dented the sides as he pushed the vehicle in as far as it would go.

Wedged between two trees, he unrolled a back window, shut off the engine, and climbed out. He tossed the keys as far as he could. Removing a Motorola radio from his pocket, he pressed the button.

"This is Hugh. I'm calling for someone in range of the peak."

"I'm in range," a familiar voice responded.

"How far out are you?"

"About fifteen minutes. Hang tight."

"10-4. I have some work to do yet," Hugh said and took out his mini flashlight and went to the front of the car. "No need to rush."

"Drop complete?"

"Yeah. But I'm deep," Hugh said and looked out from where he came. "I don't know how long it's going to take me to get back out by foot."

"Radio me when there," the voice said. "The engine will be running."

"10-4."

Hugh reached into his pocket and pulled out his multi-tool. Flipping through the options, he found the Phillips-head screwdriver and worked on removing the license plate.

31
CAGE MATCH

Tammy was the first to stir. She groaned and coughed. The back of her head still bled. She sat up dizzy and rested the club in her lap.

Daniel stirred, too. He picked up his knife and saw the woman across from him and the club in her lap.

He looked at the campsite, felt the lump on the side of his head, and looked at his hand. Blood covered his fingertips from the gash on the side of his head. He stood up with the knife, looked at the woman and the campsite, and revisited his injuries and her weapon again.

Tammy stood. She was unsure what she saw in this guy's eyes and why she was lying in this clearing with him—and why they were now waking together. Someone had placed a weapon next to her, and her first fleeting thought was of the man who had squeezed her neck. Instinct made her pick up the club and watch the young man through distrustful eyes.

Was he in on this?

Daniel looked at the White River and then charged the woman. As he neared, she swung and connected with the side of his head.

Clunk.

He fell down, and the knife fell from his grasp. Reality blinked in and out in a wave of darkness and light, and when he tried to focus, the campsite spun around him.

"What are you doing?" Tammy said.

Daniel shook his head and started to crawl. Tammy kicked him in the ribs and he gasped and rolled on his side, coughing. His head bled badly.

She lifted the club over her head. "I asked you why you're doing this."

Daniel looked to see where his knife might have gone, and the woman pulled the club back even farther, ready to smack it across his head again. "Don't even think about it," she cautioned.

Gurgle.

Tammy turned and looked in the eyes of the beast that had killed her family. She stood there, a scream held down so deep inside it had no chance of ever coming out.

Daniel got up, grabbed his knife, ran behind the woman, and stabbed her in the back. She gasped, and the monster returned to the water.

Falling forward, Daniel jumped on top of Tammy. In a fit of rage, he began to stab her and soon started hacking off pieces of her body, tossing what he could into the White River.

32

MURDERER?

Officer Hassett, Marty, and Rick Hisster could see the glow of a campfire ahead. Someone occupied the circular cutout, and they were going to stop by to see how the campers were doing.

Loud grunts could be heard over the roar of the river, and Officer Hassett drew his weapon and ran toward the firelight. Both Marty and Rick followed at a safe distance.

"Get off of her now!" Officer Hassett ordered, his weapon firmly grasped in interlaced hands, his feet apart so his balance and aim were solid. "Drop the knife and get off of her, Daniel!"

Marty and Rick moved in close enough to see a boy on his knees with a knife in his hand. He was panting like a wild animal, covered in blood, and straddling what appeared to have been a woman.

"Drop the knife or I'm going to shoot!"

Daniel looked at the officer, at Tammy, at the water, and then tossed another of her body parts into the river. He dropped the knife, and Officer Hassett holstered his weapon and charged the boy, knocking him off the severely desecrated corpse.

Officer Hassett pinned the boy to the ground, cuffed him, and grabbed for the radio attached to his shoulder.

"Dispatch, please send all available units to the White River cutout campsite," Officer Hassett said, out of breath. "You're going to need to send a CSI unit out here, too."

Marty ran in and stood over the boy and looked down on him. He smacked him.

"Is this what you did to my officer?"

Officer Hassett grabbed Marty's arm, and Marty shrugged him off.

"I asked you a question, boy!" Marty slapped him again.

"Stop it," Officer Hassett said and pulled Marty away from Daniel. "Don't bother doing that. The boy is mute and severely slow."

Something in the water caught Rick Hisster's attention, and he walked to the shoreline, oblivious to what Marty and Craig Hassett were doing.

"You can hit him all day long," Officer Hassett said. "He will never answer you."

"Dammit," Marty said and looked down on the woman. Her face was caved in, and she was missing an arm. Hunks of flesh were missing, and the rest of her body was hacked up badly. "Could this be him?"

"Who?" Officer Hassett said. "The person that made all those people disappear?"

The officer sat there, covered in blood, and looked in the opposite direction of the river. "I never would have thought that until today."

33

NO EVIDENCE

Johnny Phatz pulled up next to Hugh, and Hugh handed the cabbie the license plates from the California car.

"Ain't nobody finding her in there," Hugh said. "I wedged her in there good, and then I took a little extra time to cover her up with some of the bush lying around."

"You going to stand out there all night or do you want to head back and talk on the way?"

Hugh tapped the roof of the car and walked around the front and climbed into the passenger seat.

"I'm just happy we caught some today."

"How many?" Johnny asked and began to drive.

"There were four of them. Mom, Dad, and two teenagers."

"Four is a good number."

Hugh nodded. "It should keep them quiet for a day or two."

"Do you think the others did their part?"

Hugh hung his arm out of the open window. "I got confirmation back on the radio so I couldn't see why not."

"But you're not sure?"

Hugh looked at Johnny. "How could I be sure? I sent them upriver, and I got a call back. If that's verification, then yeah, I'm sure."

"It sounds like you're as sure about this as I was when they arrested me. I knew they wouldn't be able to keep me in long because you can't hold a man when there's no evidence. The FBI thinks they

109

can come to Newport and try and take what is ours . . . invade our land."

"We won't let them."

"No, Uncle Hugh, we never will."

"We need more."

"We have to see how the rest of what happened today played out."

"I know," Hugh said and lifted his hand and moved it through the air like a snake, playing in the wind. "Just like I know there'll always be more."

"I collected all the debris that washed up. I put it in the trunk."

"Can any of it be reused?"

"A couple life vests and paddles and I believe one helmet." He looked at his uncle. "Everything else is no good."

"Keep your eyes on the road. It's dark up here, and we don't need any deer jumping across our way and you're looking at me and you go swerving into a tree or something because it scares the crap out of you. I can hear you just fine when you're looking at the road."

"The raft is in shreds and the helmets and rest of the vests all have claw marks in them."

"We'll burn them. While I'm thinking about it, we need more guts and blood. I used the last of it today. Whatever you made last time, do that again. They seem to love it."

"That's easy enough. I'll take the boys hunting tomorrow."

34

A FEELING

Floating in the dark, fast-moving water, the eyes were just above the waterline, transfixed on the image of another meal that walked too close to the river's edge. The man glowed in the flicker of the firelight behind him.

Sinking to the bottom, the beast used the power of its muscular legs to propel forward like a dart through the water. Once it got to the shallows, it moved quickly. It stood, hurried through the ankle-deep water, and grabbed the man by his mouth with one hand and took hold of his shoulders with the other.

The beast gave the neck a quick twist, and the body went limp. The head barely remained on the body as the beast dove back into the water, taking its kill down to the bottom.

Webbed feet kicked; the current had no authority over the strength of the river monster. Toward its den it paddled with more bounty.

"Where did Rick go?" Marty said and looked around. He had to step out from where he was to get a look at the water's edge because the tent blocked the view. The man was nowhere in sight.

Officer Hassett shrugged. "He's probably pacing his property line, having a damn anxiety attack knowing all these people are coming and are going to use his property as a segue to get here."

Marty would have laughed if there wasn't a mauled woman between his feet along with a young man who had somehow gone mad. He saw that

Officer Hassett had taken off his uniform shirt and was using it to press on the wound on the side of Daniel's head.

If this kid was responsible for killing all those people, Marty would like to take the kid's head and run it through a grinder. Challenged or not, his friend was dead and so was her family, and he had to live with the fact that he sent her out here alone to face a lion that looked like a kitten.

"The newspapers are going to dub him the White River Killer," Marty said. "I can see it already. They're going to make a spectacle out of him."

"I've known this young man since before he started to walk," Officer Hassett said. "I can't believe he was capable of doing such a thing."

Marty turned and looked at the water. Thinking like a policeman always meant there were other reasons or motives at play. Especially when it felt like this wasn't the answer. "Well maybe he wasn't."

Hassett looked over his shoulder. "What does that mean?"

"It can mean a lot of things, Officer. You just have to figure that out." Marty stared at the sloshing White River as if the answer was somewhere out there rather than in the chaos underneath his feet. It was a hunch. "It seemed the kid was deliberately throwing those body parts into the river."

"So what if he was?"

Marty turned away. "Yeah, I didn't think much of it either. Then I started to think maybe he was trying to feed something."

Officer Hassett said something, but Marty couldn't hear his reply because the reinforcements had arrived and they were coming in droves. Marty chose a stump and sat, knowing his sneakers had trace evidence all over them. He would have to give a statement as to what he saw, too. He had run crime scenes a billion times and knew the drill. But this one he believed trailed out into that water there, too. That unassuming opening was the maw to something evil and out of someone's worst nightmare, and it had a constant washer to keep it clean of any trace evidence.

35

ROUNDTABLE

"Did you think Daniel was capable of killing the woman?" news anchor Hannah Dober asked.

Officer Craig Hassett, dressed in his uniform, leaned forward and rested his elbow on the table. He shook his head. "Never. I've known Daniel since he was a young child. I know problems began between the Happ parents as soon as his mental handicaps became apparent. I'd been called to the house numerous times because of the parents fighting. His father soon left, and the mother struggled alone to raise a mute boy with a mental disability."

Jules Zimmardo interrupted. "As far as I'm concerned, his mental deficiencies don't absolve him of his horrific crime."

"I didn't say they did," Officer Hassett said, and his tone had a bite to it.

"Right now, there is one murder we can prove he committed, but we can't identify the victim because she was so badly bludgeoned," Jules said. "Of course my curious mind wanders to the possibility that he had something to do with the six people who went missing."

"I think we can go around in circles about whether or not Daniel deserves mercy because of his disability or if he deserves to be tried as a fit adult," Hannah said, taking control of the conversation. "Let's put that aside and allow a judge to decide that. I'd like to switch our attention to a special guest who has a completely different take on what might have happened or has been happening at the White River in Newport."

A frail man came onto the screen. His hair was a mess, and the thick eyeglasses he wore made his eyes look huge.

"Doctor Stephen Hughes is a cryptozoologist and has studied in the field for over thirty-five years. Welcome, Doctor Hughes, and thanks for coming on our program."

Dr. Hughes nodded his head. "Thank you for having me."

"Let's start by explaining exactly what it is you do," Hannah said.

"I search for animals whose existence has not been proven due to lack of evidence. The animals I generally study are called cryptids. Most of the time, cryptids appear in folklore, legends, and mythology. Well-known examples of cryptids the audience can grasp would include the Yeti in the Himalayas, the Loch Ness Monster in Scotland, and of course Sasquatch right here in North America."

"Doctor, you were given special privilege to study the location in which this horrific crime took place, is that correct?"

"After I expressed an interest because I was drawn to the events that took place at the White River, I did ask for special permission to look at the crime scene and evidence collected."

"Can you tell the audience what it is about that location that brought you here?" Hannah opened her hands as she spoke.

"There were quite a few things I noticed and pieced together that led me to believe that there may be some validity behind the White River Monster legend and that Daniel was not acting alone."

Jules Zimmardo rolled her eyes. "You have to be kidding me. The White River Monster?"

"Yes, the White River Monster," Dr. Hughes said.

"Not one stitch of evidence has ever been found that this creature, or monster as the legend says, even exists."

"New species of fish are being discovered and documented every day," Dr. Hughes said. "Why would it be so unbelievable to think there might be an undiscovered cryptid right here in Newport?"

"The answer is simple, Doctor. It's because thousands of people have looked for this thing for over a hundred years, and no one has brought forth a shred of evidence."

"I believe there was evidence all around that crime scene."

"Oh really? I've reviewed the crime scene photos, and I don't see anything but chaos and a mind that snapped."

"You're not looking at the photographs with an objective eye. You don't see the things that I do."

Jules laughed and looked away.

"Laugh all you want," Dr. Hughes said.

"We don't need to be rude to each other," Hannah said. "A respectful debate is what you were all invited here for."

"I'm not bothered by her ridicule," Dr. Hughes said. "I wouldn't be surprised if some sort of evidence comes forward within the next week. Things are going to show up that the police missed during their investigation."

"What do you think they missed?" Hannah said.

"That there was a slow, mute young man who spent most of his time in a forest, alone. He was an expert trapper, and in one of the photographs I noticed that there was a gutted raccoon on top of a large rock or boulder alongside the river."

"And that proves what?" Jules said.

"Hold on and let him answer the question," Hannah said.

"It proves that Daniel was feeding something. I believe he had a bond with it."

"I find your theories to be a bit out there," Officer Hassett said. "Do you forget that there's cutthroat, rainbow, brown, and brook trout all throughout the river?"

"I know what species of fish occupy the White River," Dr. Hughes said. "What I'm saying is I believe that there is a monster that is active in that part of the river, and it's not acting alone."

Officer Hassett looked at Jules and then at Hannah. Sarcasm seeped into his next comment. "So the natives are feeding it, petting it, taking it for a walk?"

"Mockery aside, Officer Hassett, I believe they are feeding it, yes."

"So let me get this straight," Jules said. "You think the White River Monster is real because some slow young man who likes to trap animals and dissect them at the river's edge and toss the guts into the water, snaps for reasons unknown, bludgeons a woman, and tosses her body parts into the water to feed a monster?"

"That's right."

"And let me guess. Your theory suggests that the six missing people might have met the same fate?"

"It seems like a logical conclusion to me," Dr. Hughes said and pushed his glasses up.

Jules tried to hide her laugh behind her hand, and Officer Hassett leaned back in his chair. "I'm kind of with Jules here. Daniel trapped animals and liked to use them to feed the fish in the river. That's it. That doesn't constitute you getting on national television and claiming that the White River Monster exists. Don't you think that's a little irresponsible?"

Dr. Hughes shook his head. "I don't think that's irresponsible at all if I believe what I'm telling is the truth. I truly believe it is out there. It is the where that escapes me."

"Of course it escapes you the same way it has escaped all of those who have come before you."

"I believe the creature respires through its skin and can live in water and on dry land—kind of like a croc—and I believe it has been occupying the area for a long time and knows how to hide."

"How long are you suggesting this creature has been here in Newport, Doctor?" Hannah said.

"I'm thinking the creature may have occupied the area since the early 1500s."

Jules stared with a sudden interest, and Officer Hassett grabbed his chin as his eyes volleyed between Hannah and Dr. Hughes.

"That's quite a claim," Hannah said. "What brings you to that time period and why?"

"Quite simply, Hernando de Soto was a Spanish conquistador who happened to be passing through Newport on or around October 22, 1541. There was a letter delivered, referring to his journey into Newport."

Dr Hughes reached into a coat pocket, withdrew a folded piece of paper, and fixed his glasses again. He unfolded the page and read.

"They went down the Rocky Bayou to Guion, which is among some rugged mountains next to a river . . . the White River. It went on to say that a little less than a dozen of his men went missing, along with some of their pillaged gold."

Hannah looked at Jules and Officer Hassett. "I'm sorry, I'm not following."

"Newport was well populated, and people hid from de Soto. He was a feared man and well received into Newport for fear of what he might do if treated otherwise. The question that I ask myself is not who took the men and his gold, but what? No man or even group of men would have challenged de Soto."

Thump. Thump. Thump.

Marty Mallow turned off the television set and went to his door.

Thump.

He yanked the door open and wondered what the fuss was about. Joan Hisster was at his door. Her face was pale, and worry had settled in her distant gaze.

"I haven't seen Rick in two days," Joan said. "I think something bad might have happened to him."

36

GONE MISSING

Marty invited Joan inside, and he sat her down at the table for fear that she might fall over. She was breathing heavily—near hyperventilating—and a terrible tremble made her unsteady. Marty wondered how she even made it over here.

"Did you call the police?"

"Of course I did," Joan said and gasped. "They're not interested because Rick has gone wandering off before only to come home confused." She bit down on her bottom lip.

"You need to calm down so we can talk and figure this out," Marty said and went to the sink. He filled up a glass of water and had Joan drink it. He sat in the chair next to her and rubbed her back. "Let's not talk until you're calm enough."

Joan nodded, and Marty already started to put some of the pieces together. But he would wait for Joan to find calm so he could get cohesive answers and build a time line. This would allow him to validate the first thought that came screaming into his head.

Fifteen minutes went by before her breathing returned to normal, but the shaking remained. If he had a Valium, he would give her one just to help her through this moment.

"When did you say Rick didn't come home?" Marty said.

"Two nights ago." Her words came out fast.

"Joan," Marty said with a soft voice. "I need you to look at me."

Joan looked with bright red eyes and huge pupils.

"I did this for a living for a very long time. I need you to stay calm and trust in me. Be precise with your answers, and try not to leave out any details. That could be the difference in understanding where he went or not. Do you understand me?"

"Yes," Joan said and bounced a knee.

"What happened before he disappeared?"

Joan looked at him, lost. "I don't know what you mean."

"Did you two have an argument? Did he tell you where he was going? Did he take the car or did he walk?"

"We had an argument," Joan said. "He wanted to go outside and pick things up around the property, and I didn't want him to do that. His OCD can be so annoying, and it gets in the way of our everyday life. That day I had had enough."

"OK," Marty said. "This is all good information for helping us to understand where he went."

"Ever since he returned home from war, his OCD seemed to worsen. He stood outside and protected the property like he was protecting his barracks in Afghanistan. He said if he was more diligent while he was overseas he could have saved the lives of his friends who died in a bombing."

Marty bit down hard. That explained what the man was always doing looking over his property, chasing people off of it like a rabid dog.

"The last time I saw him was when I looked out the window. He was talking with you and Officer Hassett. He never came home that night."

"He never came home?"

Joan shook her head, and Marty thought back to that night.

"I didn't know where he went. I thought he might have still been with you, or maybe Officer Hassett took him in because I know you guys saw what happened in the cutout."

"How do you know he was in the cutout?"

"I saw the direction you guys walked in." Joan picked at her fingers. "If it was as half as bad as the news said, maybe it triggered a buried PTSD event or something. I don't know how this stuff works. So I called the VA, and he hadn't been in."

"Come," Marty said. "You've told me everything I need to know. Let me walk you home. I want you to let me have a look around, and I'll get back to you."

Joan took his hand and stood. Her legs were a lot more stable now that she had calmed some.

"Please try to get some rest. If you're going to be up and about, all you're going to do is worry. Do you have something you can take to help you sleep?"

Joan nodded. "Marty has a stockpile of medicine. I hit it every now and then to help me sleep when I need it."

"I think you need it," Marty said and escorted Joan home.

37

CAPTAIN

Marty left Joan and walked to the rear of the Hissters' property. There was a clear trail formed where people traveled to gain access to the cutout. Marty purposely stayed off the path, and as he walked, he looked at the ground around his feet.

He walked slowly and deliberately, each footfall a purposeful placement. He scanned the ground around his feet. He stopped a few times to look at something that had an off color or didn't look like it belonged to the landscape. So far, he hadn't turned anything up.

Undiscouraged, he kept his pace and watched where he stepped. Less than ten feet away from the cutout, a gleam, reflected for a fraction of a second made him stop. His body was stiff as he got down to one knee, brushed aside the fallen leaves, and picked up a cell phone. The gleam had come from the glass screen.

"Ailish," Marty said, and a chill rocked his body. He didn't need to turn it on to know the phone had belonged to her because he had issued it to her. This confirmed that she had made it to the cutout—and likely so did her sister. The only question that remained was what happened to them.

Marty stepped into the cutout and looked around. There was no indication that a gruesome murder had taken place there only two days ago. Everything had been documented, tagged, bagged, and hauled away. That included Daniel Happ and the unidentified woman that had been bludgeoned beyond recognition and even possibly identification.

Then a thought crept into his mind.

"I truly believe it is out there."

That's what he had heard Dr. Hughes say before Joan Hisster pounded on his door. Now that he reflected on the night of the murder, that theory the doctor laid out made more sense than ever. Rick had been at the shoreline looking into the water. Marty had felt something wasn't right and he looked to see where Rick was, but he was gone like he had never even been there.

Marty walked to the water's edge and looked into the river. Whatever this thing was, it lived somewhere near here. He didn't know that for sure and was only surmising, but if he were a betting man, he'd ante up his entire earnings on that supposition.

He closed his eyes and turned his face into the wind. Taking a deep breath, he sighed. He was afraid to tell Joan what he believed happened to her husband. For now, he would say he was following up on leads and leave it at that. Like Dr. Hughes, he was merely acting on a hunch.

Stuffing the cell phone into his pocket, he scanned the area and saw something that lapped against the shoreline about twenty feet away. White in color and almost blended into the shoreline rocks, he walked to it and picked it up. It was a padded rafting helmet. Scratched up and clearly used, the name 'White River Rentals' was written on the side of it in black magic marker.

Marty decided he would take it to the company because he knew the biggest leads came from the smallest, most obscure finds.

38

WHITE RIVER RENTALS

Marty tossed the helmet into the passenger seat, plugged 'White River Rentals' into his navigation system, and hit go. The route was relatively straight; about seven miles upriver. In his short time living in the area, he had never heard of the rental company.

He drove his four-wheel drive Ford Expedition to the instructed destination and saw he was second in line. A flashy, expensive vehicle was pulled aside, and two men dressed in button-down shirts and khaki pants looked like they were ready for a meeting rather than a whitewater adventure.

An old man held a finger up to Marty, and he just watched things unfold in a comical way. The old man pulled out a raft large enough for four people, and he set the tip in the water in a man-made slip. Marty watched him talk to the two men, hand them equipment, and wait until they put it on. He handed them their paddles and watched them set off down the river.

The old man erected a fence that blocked the slip and then retrieved something from inside the cage he had taken the raft out of. Then he went to the exact spot where the men launched. He worked there for a moment, returned whatever he had gotten out of the cage, possibly locked it, and took down the makeshift fence and walked to Marty's car.

"May I help you?"

Marty reached over and grabbed the helmet and handed it to the old man.

"I found it on the shore downriver."

"This one looks like it was dragged across the rocks and spit out onto the shore."

"It sure does. The name's Marty."

"Hugh," the old man said. He held up the helmet. "Thank you. One among many. I appreciate you returning it to me."

"No problem," Marty said and noticed Hugh had a smell about him that he knew all too well. He smelled like death . . . or more like the gore of a crime scene. He thought he could smell blood. Although the smell was unmistakable, the scent of the forest and that which the wind carried around with it helped to mask it.

"Where did you say you found it?" Hugh said and held up the helmet.

"Not too far away from where that murder took place, I'm afraid."

Hugh shook his head. "That's a real tragedy. I've seen that boy around these parts for years. I was shocked to come to find out it was him."

Marty put his vehicle in reverse but kept his foot on the brake.

"You may have two more helmets washing ashore," Marty said with a smile.

"Why do you say that?" Hugh said, obviously not getting it.

"Those two men looked like they belonged in a conference room, not a raft."

Hugh smiled. "My sentiments exactly, but they refused a ride-on guide. They sign the release, I say OK. I just don't get some people."

"Me neither," Marty said. "Say, listen, did you know that boy to be violent in any way?"

"No," Hugh said. "At least not toward people. Passive, if I had to choose a word."

"Any reason you could think of that might send him to do something like that?"

"What, to murder people?" Hugh shrugged. "The need to survive? Maybe he felt threatened by them people."

Marty caught the scent again. Hugh smelled of blood.

"There was no 'them.' It was only one woman. Take care, Hugh," Marty said and pulled away. He didn't hesitate or look back because he didn't want Hugh to know what he suspected. What that man just did was slip up.

As he drove back toward his place he noticed that the raft rental shack was about a mile before the cutout the cab drivers used to drop the people off.

Things were becoming interesting, and a bigger picture was beginning to develop for Marty—one that needed to be followed up on immediately if he were to fully understand what was going here in Newport, Arkansas.

PREPARING

The river ride started out slow enough, and the men looked at each other with an accomplished laugh.

"I appreciate you taking me out here," Johnny Strife said to the man to his left. He was taking spray to the face, and water dumped into his lap. "It is a much needed break from the office and having to make all these decisions and deals."

"You're welcome," Donald Cory said with a laugh.

"What?" Johnny said.

"You love the power of having these people crawling to you in droves, begging to be recognized. The industry is just clogged with them. Writers will sell their souls to get recognized, and you know it. The mighty Harnes & Roble bookstore. The last of the mortar and brick big guys loves to play them games with the little guys. Put them in their place."

Johnny smiled, and that soon turned into a laugh.

"And look at you!" Johnny fired back. "You're the book buyer to the largest retail chain ever. You have people like me willing to eat the shit off the bottom of your shoes to get my stuff into your stores. I mean the amount of people that come into your establishment—"

"Well you're past that point, Johnny. You're here in our home state, and you're a special guest. You don't have to eat the shit. You've earned your way in. That's why we're here. I'll take some of what you have and make you a superstar in your company.

Let's keep the big six in place, but give me your best. I don't want some no-name who thinks he's a King or a Koontz. Let those hungry bastards kick at the door all day. All we have to do is ignore them. That's our job."

"I'll let them kick, and you'll get my best," Johnny said. "I won't screw this deal up, and I want to thank you for the opportunity."

"No problem," Donald said. "And remember something, Johnny. As long as our glass is full, we don't have to worry about the losers crawling at our feet, begging for a sip."

Just then, a rogue wave smashed into the side of the raft and flipped it over. Both men were tossed into the choppy water, which pulled them under, dragged them along, and only allowed them back up every now and then for a breath of air.

They banged into a submerged boulder and tried to swim for the shore in a desperate attempt to survive. Miraculously, the river let them go, and both men made it and found themselves facedown next to the river; their legs flopped around in the current, their breath gone in heavy gasps. The water they'd swallowed made their stomachs bulge against the wet ground.

Johnny sat up and watched the paddles and raft float away. "What now?"

"We stay to the shoreline and walk our way back to where that little cabin hut thing is. Thank God I put all my personal stuff in that lock-box. We'll stop at a store and get new, dry clothes before we head back and sign the deal."

"Sounds like a good plan."

Both men stood, winded from their fight with the current, and started to walk back to the hut, their clothing hugging their bodies.

Crack.

They froze and looked behind them in the forest. There was nothing there but fallen limbs and a floor covered with a thick layer of leaves.

"Come on, let's keep moving," Donald said. "There's probably wildlife all up and down the bank that feeds off the fish. Let's not get ourselves worried over a silly sound."

"You're right," Johnny said, still sticking to the script to ensure he kept the deal.

40

WHITE RIVER MONSTERS

The men resumed their journey back to the shack where their adventure started. Five minutes ago they were on top of the world, talking about how they stuck it to the little guy and enjoyed doing so. Now, with their professional attire clinging to their bodies, their breath heavy and bodies tired and bloated and bruised from the struggle against the river's might, they were both quiet and feeling like one of those little guys. When your mortality comes into question, they realized, it can humble you quickly.

There was no corporate food chain for them to reign over out here; there was just a palpable concern that they'd just stared tragedy in the face and barely came out alive.

Crack!

The sound boomed on and off to their left. It sounded deliberate . . . as if something was stalking them and trying to scare them. They looked into the woods and at each other.

"Is there any truth to that monster legend?" Johnny asked, and his worry put a tremble into his voice.

"No," Donald said. "It was this mentally challenged guy committing those crimes. They caught him the other day. I heard someone refer to him as the White River Killer."

Crack!

Whatever made that sound made it deliberately— they were sure of it now. It was letting them know they were being followed.

"I don't like this," Donald said, his voice revealing his fear against the unknown that had started to close in around him. "Maybe we should jump back in the water and let it take us far away from here."

"OK, we can do that," Johnny said, his focus sharp, determined to escape these woods.

Gurgle.

Both men's eyes snapped forward, and they froze at what they saw. A tall, fishlike man stood in front of them on the land. Its wet skin glistened in the sunlight, and its tiny eyes stayed focused on them. The mouth was loaded with long, sharp teeth, and it had gills and tentacles that swayed back and forth like hands ready to reach out and grab them at any time.

Click. Gurgle. Click.

The sounds that came out of this creature were nothing short of frightening, and the men were paralyzed by their fear. All they could do was stand there and look at it.

Click. Click. Gurgle.

This time, the sound came from behind Johnny, and he realized the creature in front of them was communicating to one that was behind them. He dared to look, and just as he did, Johnny was shoved so hard his body slammed to the ground and he slid in the mud. By the time he was able to get to his back, the other massive primal sea creature grabbed him by his legs and picked him up and swung him around with tremendous force. His body crashed into the trunk of a massive tree, and his neck snapped to the side and everything went numb. There was very little air making it into his collapsed lungs, but there was no pain from the broken bones because of the numbness. Blood trickled out of his eyes and nose.

His hearing was gone but his eyesight, although tinted red, remained as he watched a mouth with nasty serrated teeth descend on his midsection and bite into his flesh and rip out a massive chunk.

The creature ate, and Johnny began to convulse.

The living thing that stood before Donald slowly reached out a webbed hand before it grabbed the man by his chin. It turned Donald's head from side to side as if it were appraising its catch.

"Please, no," Donald begged, and the creature pulled him close. Donald wasn't a small man by any means, but the river monster towered over him.

Gurgle.

The feasting beast behind him responded.

Click. Click.

The webbed hand squeezed Donald's face and forced his mouth open. The beast looked inside the man's stretched jaws, and Donald felt something come over his shoulder. His eyes widened when he saw that it was a tendril, and he was terrified as it moved into his mouth. Donald began to choke and dry heave on it as it pushed its way down into his stomach.

With a nasty ripping sound, the tendril came out of Donald's mouth with his stomach and parts of his larynx. Blood spilled from Donald's mouth, and the beast lapped it up with its long, flickering tongue.

Click.

The two monsters dragged their kills into the White River and disappeared into the depths.

41
PLANNING

Marty arrived at his place with a running checklist in his head. He searched around for bolt cutters, his pistol and a full magazine, holster, and his Mag light. He placed Ailish's cell phone on the table next to all the gathered items and tried to think what else he might need.

"A duffel bag," he said and snapped his fingers.

Three knocks on his door halted his search, and through the sidelight he saw Joan pacing back and forth. Marty drew a deep breath, and with his mind on other things right now, he didn't have a prepared answer that might make this woman feel at ease about her husband's whereabouts.

He opened the door and invited her in and offered her a seat. She looked like she hadn't slept a wink.

"What's all of this?" she said and stared at the pile of collected things.

"These are some of the things I need in order to help find your husband," Marty lied. He knew Rick was dead, that the White River Monster had dragged him into the cold depths of the river the night he went missing.

"Do you know where he went?"

"No, but I have an idea."

Joan perked up, the need for an answer evident in her expression.

"I think your husband might have gone looking for the six bodies that were missing. I believe he had a lot of conversations with Daniel, and he might have known the many places the young man visited. I believe your husband thought Daniel was a serial killer. 'The White River Killer,' I believe were his words."

"He hasn't had food or water . . ."

"No, but he has the military skills. I believe this is another attempt to help ease his troubled mind and earn some penance from all those people he felt responsible for."

Joan nodded her head, and a tear dripped from her eye and ran down her face. She stood, gave Marty a hug, and kissed his cheek.

"Thank you. Please be careful. I know he hasn't been the kindest person to you."

She exited the house, and Marty watched her leave with a heavy heart of his own, knowing she would never see her husband again.

42

CAGE MATCH

Hugh closed the raft rental shop at the normal time. He took from the box the keys that belonged to the two men he had sent down the river earlier in the day, got into their vehicle, and drove toward the more rural area of Newport.

Marty waited fifteen minutes before he emerged from the brush. He grasped his gun tightly in his right hand, and the flashlight blinked on, being worked by his left hand. A black duffel bag was slung over his shoulder, and it contained some miscellaneous supplies.

Entering the unsecured shack, Marty saw that the inside was small and simple, containing only a single wooden stool, the novel Tom Sawyer on a shelf below the window, and a metal lock-box with a jar filled with keys that fit the lock on the box. There was a toilet hidden behind a curtain that looked as though it hadn't been cleaned since it was installed.

Exiting the shack, Marty swept the area with the beam of his flashlight and came upon the fenced-in rafts. Two were piled on top of each other, and each looked brand new. Paddles were in a trash can with holes drilled out toward the bottom to allow rain water to drain away. Life vests and helmets hung on hooks in pairs and were sorted by size. The one Marty had dropped off earlier in the day was nowhere to be seen.

Marty lowered the light and took a moment to pay attention to his senses: the sound of the river, the feel of the breeze caressing his skin, the smell of the fresh water—it was interrupted by something foul. It was the same smell Hugh had reeked of, and it was exactly what Marty was looking for.

He raised the flashlight beam and pointed into the corner of the fenced-in equipment. There was space back there for something, but Marty couldn't see what it was. The vegetation that encompassed the back half of the cage inhibited him from just walking around it. He was forced to place his duffel bag on the ground, holster his weapon, and grab the bolt cutters.

The lock snapped easily, and Marty dropped the bolt cutters, tossed the broken lock into the river, and took control of his weapon again. Using caution as he approached, when he reached the back of the cage, he saw that there was a garbage can with a lid bungeed down. He pulled away the bungee and lifted the lid off the garbage can.

The smell hit Marty and he staggered away, feeling bile climb up his throat, but he was able to hold it down.

He held the flashlight with his teeth and took a rag out of his pocket and covered his nose and mouth with it. He returned to the can and saw that it was a giant bucket of blood and guts. A smaller pail sat next to the large can.

Marty covered everything back up and leaned on one of the rafts and thought for a moment.

What did all of this mean? How was Hugh connected to this, and who else was involved? It was to this can filled with blood that Hugh had gone right after the men had launched and he had erected the makeshift fence to block Marty's view. Marty then approached the launch ramp a second time, bent down, and returned to the cage.

He felt that the answer was right under his nose, but he couldn't figure it out. He needed a little time to think things through. Gathering his supplies,

Marty hurried to get out of there before someone came by and saw him.

43

REINFORCEMENTS

During his trip back to his house, Marty was given plenty of time to think about what the things he saw meant, and he had a very good idea what Hugh was doing and what that meant for the six missing people and Dr. Hughes. As unbelievable as his thoughts were, he truly felt he needed to follow through with his plan to stop it.

Once he got inside the house, he picked up Ailish's phone and turned it on. Thankful for weatherproofing and long-lasting battery cells for agents in the field, Marty sighed in relief as the phone lit up. He called Agent Roger Pokorny.

"Ailish?" Roger said. There was doubt in the way he said her name.

"It's Marty."

"Marty. You found Ailish's phone?"

"Among other things," Marty said. "I have a good understanding of what's going on here, Roger. I need you to speak to the new captain and send two dozen men—more, if he can spare them. Make sure everyone comes armed. No pistols. Automatic weapons. They have to be automatic. We need patrol boats from our nearest base brought here."

"Slow down, Marty," Roger said. "You're spitting an awful lot at me, and you're speaking so fast I can't even take these notes down."

"I don't have time for slow, Roger. I'm in my house and fearing for my safety. If anyone knows what I'm up to, I could find myself in a world of trouble. My gun will not be leaving my hand tonight, do you understand that?"

"Yes."

"Good, now make sure we have a half dozen sets of scuba gear arrive with the boats. You got it?"

"I got it, and I'll get on it."

"Right away, Roger. Call the captain now. This can't wait till morning. We need to get you guys in transit now. Our guys. I don't know how deep things run around here and who I can trust."

"OK, Marty. I'm calling him now. We'll be there soon. You hang in there."

"I have another important call to make. Please get me the phone number to a Dr. Stephen Hughes. He's a cryptozoologist. He's popular in that community, and I believe he's still here in Newport."

After a few moments, Roger gave Marty the doctor's phone number.

"Thank you, Roger."

"No problem. Are you sure you're going to be OK?"

"I'll make it until you get here. Work fast like you just did, and everything will be just fine."

Marty hung up the phone and called Dr. Hughes.

"Doctor Stephen Hughes."

"Doctor Hughes, this is Special Agent Marty Mallow. I am here in Newport, Arkansas investigating the disappearances of the six individuals and the reason why the young man Daniel was driven to murder."

"You saw me on the television this morning?" Dr. Hughes said.

"I did. I believe you are one hundred percent correct in your assessment of this region of the White River. I would like you to come and meet me as soon as you can. I live in a home right next to ground zero."

"Directions, please. I'll come at first light."

Marty gave the doctor his address and specific directions on how to get there. He hung up the phone and settled in a seat, distracted by a random thought. Why did the taxi driver drop people off at that spot? Why so far away?

"To tire them out?" Marty said aloud. "To make sure they crossed paths with the Flowers and the Hissters?"

He opened his hands and stood.

"Why did Rick Hisster hate Nick and Marsha Flowers so much?"

The answer was in there somewhere, but where eluded him for the moment.

"Let me start with Hugh," Marty said and shut out all the lights in his house. "He was a part of this puzzle and possibly the easiest one to figure out. He took those guys' vehicle. He was getting rid of it."

He looked out the corner of his drawn shades to see if anyone was on to him. All he saw was darkness. It was going to be a long night.

44

TO PROVE A LEGEND

Thump, thump, thump.

Marty jumped out of the seat he had fallen asleep in and pointed the gun at a blurry table. Dull light beamed in through the gaps in the shade, indicating that a new day had arrived.

Thump, thump.

"Marty? It's Doctor Hughes, are you in there?"

Marty rubbed his eyes, tried to straighten himself, and focused on the clock. It was 6 a.m. His head buzzed, having been jarred from a deep sleep, but he needed to get himself together and quickly.

He went to the door and opened it.

"Please, Doctor, come in."

The doctor removed his hat and stepped inside. "Thank you." He offered Marty his hand.

"It is a pleasure to meet you in person, Doctor," Marty said and shook his hand. "Can I get you anything? Perhaps a cup of coffee?"

"No thank you. I'm sorry I've come at such an early hour, but your call had me up most of the night, curious to what you might know of this White River Monster."

"Perhaps a walk?" Marty suggested.

"Certainly."

Marty checked his gun, pushed it into its holster, and made sure he had a spare clip. "Please, follow me."

The two men walked the path to the cutout.

"Ah, I recognize this as the camping spot where Daniel murdered that woman," Dr. Hughes said.

"You are correct. This is where Daniel killed the Jane Doe. I saw it with my own eyes. It was horrific, and I've seen some pretty horrible things to compare it to."

"That's what the pictures showed." Dr. Hughes looked at Marty. "Why did you bring me here?"

"I brought you here because this is a location where the river monster comes on land. Like a croc."

Dr. Hughes blinked hard and looked at the opening and at the fast rushing body of water. "You said that as a matter of fact."

"Yes, I did."

The doctor continued to look out into the water and moved to the shoreline so that just the tips of his shoes would get wet. He put on his hat.

"That night, when the young man killed that woman, three of us came into this camp to see what was going on. There was all this noise." Marty licked his lips. "Officer Hassett, a man named Rick Hisster, and I saw what Daniel was doing, and Officer Hassett intervened. But before he could stop him, Daniel threw pieces of the woman's body into the river as if he were trying to feed something."

"What are you suggesting he was feeding?"

"I'm not suggesting he was trying to feed anything at all actually," Marty said.

"But you said—"

"I said 'as if' he was trying to feed something. That's the way it appeared. Now that I have had time to think about it, reflect on the things you said on TV, I believe he was letting the monster know there was food for him."

"Like putting chum in the water?"

"Just like that," Marty said. "But it doesn't stop there. After we got Daniel subdued, Officer Hassett and I started having a conversation about what we had just witnessed. Rick Hisster was doing his own thing, but I'm not sure exactly what. It was dark out, and there was a campfire going. Lighting wasn't the greatest, and we couldn't rely on our ears to hear anything unusual because of the sound of the rushing water. Rick had been standing right where you are now, but when I went to look to find him he was gone."

"I'm listening."

"I asked Officer Hassett where he might have gone, and he just brushed it off as Rick just having turned around and gone home. Rick was a little bit of a strange character after all, so I didn't question it that much."

"What happened, Marty?"

"Yesterday, his wife, Joan, came to my house and said her husband hadn't come home since that night. She was hysterical."

"Hmm," Dr. Hughes said and rubbed his chin. "Are you suggesting he was pulled into the water by this monster?"

"I am. The man didn't just walk away, and he certainly didn't just disappear into thin air. Something took him away."

"You know what that means, don't you?"

"That whatever it is, it lives close to this cutout."

The doctor walked the circle, looking at the stumps. "I immediately found the location of this alleged camping site to be peculiar. It's man made. But talking with you now fills in some gaps for me." The doctor sat on a stump. "I'll have to agree with you and say I think you found the monster's game trail. If that's the case, then we have to figure out how to catch the elusive creature and prove its existence."

Marty's lips curved into a smile. "I think I already have that figured out. Come, let's get back to my place. I'm expecting some friends, and they should be arriving any minute now."

45

PREPARATION IS EVERYTHING

Roger and nearly three dozen men assembled with everything Marty had requested. Marty's side yard looked like a parking lot, and men dressed in camouflage toting automatic rifles patrolled the area.

The decision makers, who included Marty, Roger, Dr. Hughes, and Officer Hassett, were gathered in Marty's dining room. His table had a detailed map opened on its surface, and that was where they planned their moves.

"I think it beneficial that the local police should be used to keep any civilians from entering the area," Marty said and looked at Officer Hassett. "Do you agree?"

"Yes."

"Excellent. You can head that up."

Officer Hassett nodded.

"Next, we launch the boats from the raft rental shack slip," Marty said. "There is a large garbage can filled with blood and guts that they've been dumping into the waters after the rafts leave the launch site."

"What about the man who runs the shack?" Roger asked, glancing around.

"I'll have one of my men arrest him and get him into custody," Officer Hassett said. "He's easy enough to find. He's either at the bar or the rental shack.

"Perfect."

"We will need one of the men to chum the water once we get the power boats in the water. I say he dumps it all in so we have a better chance of drawing this thing out."

"Agreed," a few men said at the same time.

"We will have two divers to a boat, four men per boat total. That leaves us with eight men on land. Each gunman should have a tranquilizer or bullet option. We will leave what type of shot is taken up to each agent." Marty looked at Dr. Hughes. "Would you like to take over from here?"

"Certainly," Dr. Hughes said. "Here is the cutout where most of the incidents seem to have taken place." He pointed to the exact area on the map. "From the flow of the water, I would offer a firm, educated guess that the monster has a lair on the opposite side of the river, somewhere up before the bend." The doctor stood upright. "It is safe to say that this lair is going to be well hidden, as this monster has been able to avoid detection for hundreds of years. Make no mistake: it is there—we just have to find it. Be mindful that this monster will stop at nothing to protect its home. Every agent and police officer needs to know to protect themselves at all times, and the use of deadly force may be the only acceptable line of defense. We don't know anything about this monster other than it has a taste for human flesh."

"Let's report to the men and get situated. We have a monster to catch."

To be concluded in White River Monster VI.
Get ready for monster pandemonium!

46

DRAWING THEM OUT

Three F470 combat raiding crafts, otherwise known as Zodiacs, were launched from the raft rental slip. Immediately following all crafts entering the water, two men on the shoreline dumped a vat filled with blood and guts into the White River. The rushing water turned red and gushed downstream.

All engines remained off, and the rafts started to head downriver with four men in each raft. In each Zodiac, two combat divers were in full gear: full face masks, Draeger LAR rebreathers, breathing tubes, Flipfins in case they needed to hit land, and an air-powered spear gun apiece, each equipped with enough tranquilizers inside to take down an elephant. The other two men, as with all the men on the land, were armed with Heckler & Koch 416A5-14.5" automatic assault rifles.

These men came here to catch a monster, dead or alive, and they meant business.

Marty clicked his radio. "Are you in position, Doctor Hughes?"

"Yes," the static-interfered voice came through.

"Do you have a man with you?"

"Yes. I asked that he patrol the area," Dr. Hughes said. "There's no sense in him staring at the water with me, and I'd prefer he keep my back safe."

"10-4," Marty said. "Hang tight. The package has been placed in the water. If he's here, we've given the scent and invited him to come out and play."

"He's here, and he's going to play," Dr. Hughes said.

The river pulled the crafts along. Their rugged design made the white-capped rapids of the river seem tame.

Marty Mallow and his team launched first, but as the river would have it, he was now second behind Roger Pokorny's craft. The third boat remained close behind. All of the men kept careful watch of the surface of the water, and the tension was thick. It was one thing to know what your enemy looked like, but something completely different when everything you were doing was based on speculation.

"Be ready for anything," Marty shouted over the sound of the river. He watched the water bleeding red from the chum. "Weapons ready. Divers ready. If you need to go in, go deep and find cover from the current. Eyes all over, men. We don't know what this thing is capable of, and we might not even know what we're looking at if we do see it because Doctor Hughes believes it may very well have a fleshy tone that matches its surroundings."

"Any sign of movement down your way?" Roger called over the radio.

The radio chirped.

"Nothing yet," Dr. Hughes said, this time his voice came out clear. They had sent him to the boulder Daniel had used to gut the raccoon just outside the cutout. In one hand, he held a pair of high-powered binoculars and was supposed to scan the body of water for any signs of the monster. In the other, he held onto a voice-activated recorder for his own research. "I can see the current is starting to drag the blood this far already. This is where Marty and I believe this creature lives. Men in your vessels, be aware that he is getting the scent. You must be ready for anything."

The doctor's words created more tension. The rafts continued to be dragged along by the current. Soon, the raiding crafts approached a bend in the river, and that meant they were passing the cutout.

"Easy, gentleman," Dr. Hughes said. "I don't see anything, but something doesn't feel right."

Roger spied the water, swinging his H&K everywhere he looked. The splashing of the river was distracting and played tricks on the eyes. "Do you guys see anything?"

"Negative," the responses came down the line.

"There!" one of the boatmen shouted, and Roger caught a glimpse of the large creature that watched their approach, its eyes just above the water. Spiny rays and dorsal fins on top of the head were easy to see. Roger aimed his weapon and opened fire.

The creature dove and disappeared into the white foam, but the bullets cut through the water and anything that was inside.

"Did you see that?"

"What the hell was it?" someone said.

"I think we just found what we were looking for," Marty said.

"Chins up, gentleman. I just got my first look at something I've never seen before," Roger said, and he changed clips. "And I'm not going to lie. It's scary as shit. It has brown skin, small eyes, fish and humanoid features. It didn't look friendly. I'm not sure if I hit it or not so stay alert."

The men wielding the H&K weapons remained diligent in sweeping the water for another sighting of the monster. Tense minutes passed, but the river revealed nothing but spray and the constant sound of rushing water.

"Watch your spacing, gentleman!"

The rear vessel's engines kicked to life and backed the craft up, even against the strong current of the river.

Sudden shouts erupted from the men in the rear boat. It was chaotic, and the terror was easy to hear. Everyone in the other two boats turned around and saw the raiding craft being lifted high into the air and bent in half from two monstrous hands that gripped either side and squeezed.

The men fell out of the boat and it popped. The river monster stood with the water up to its chest, snarling at the men. It let the boat go and the engine portion sank, but the front portion was pulled down the river.

The beast didn't struggle with the strong current. It just stood there as if to get a headcount of how many had come. An ear-piercing scream erupted from the mouth filled with distorted, needle-like teeth and quieted once it disappeared into the depths.

"What the fuck was that?" one of the men said. He was near delirious.

"Keep it together!" Marty shouted. "We have men in the drink."

The men in the other two boats hurried to get a hold of the two non-divers and worked on bringing them into the craft. Marty's boat had a hold of one man, and Roger's boat the other.

Roger reached his hand out and grabbed the agent. The agent's slippery hands were already freezing cold, and he was being sucked down by the current. Roger took hold with two hands and pulled as hard as he could.

"Swing a leg over the side," Roger screamed.

The floater kicked his legs up, and Roger continued to pull, but the man didn't move.

"Help me," the man said, and for a second Roger thought the man had lost it because Roger was trying to help him. There was pure terror in the agent's eyes. That's when the monster stood with a hold on the man's other leg. It growled and pulled on the man with such force it nearly pulled Roger overboard.

"No!" Roger shouted and let the man go. He fumbled to get control of his gun.

The monster held the man above its head, and as it brought him down it tore him in half. It tossed half the man onto the vessel, and everyone on board was sprayed with his blood. The beast quickly disappeared underneath the surface.

Roger's finger finally found the trigger, and he screamed as he unloaded his clip into the murky depths. His counterparts saturated the area as well.

"What the fuck is that thing?" one of the men said. "Did you just see it tear Kevin in half?"

"What sort of animal can do that?"

"Get it together, gentleman. We are at war here, fighting for our very lives."

"That thing . . . it's a nightmare, and we're in its lair."

Marty tugged on the other floater's belt and pulled him aboard his craft.

"We wanted him out, and he's out, gentleman. This is what we came here and asked for."

"I think we need to try and draw him onto land," Roger said, and Marty nodded. "Frogmen, over."

"If you see that thing under there, shoot it," he said. "And then shoot it again and again until you know it's dead! Don't take any chances."

The men gave a thumbs up.

"Use the boulders below as cover from the current. Be safe."

They sat on the sides of the boats. They held onto their masks with one hand and their weapons with the other. They fell into the river backwards and disappeared into the raging tide, looking to take the fight below the surface.

47

ABANDONING POSTS

Officer Craig Hassett pulled up to one of his patrolmen, who was stationed outside the active zone as they had planned when they were in Marty's living room.

"Have you had any contact with anyone?" Officer Hassett said.

"No," the officer said.

"They know to stay away."

The officer nodded. "The word was put out."

"I've heard gunfire over the radio. Their shouts are filled with terror." Officer Hassett looked over his shoulder. "You can hear it in the distance."

The two men paused and listened to the sound of automatic gunfire.

The officer nodded. "I can hear it."

"It sounds like a war going on down there."

"It sure does."

"I think they might be in contact with the monster," Officer Hassett said.

"Do you think that's possible?"

"From the sound of things, it sure seems that way."

"How long until they reach land?" the officer said.

Officer Hassett looked off into the distance and considered the question. These otherwise quiet woods were now becoming a staging area between man and monster.

"Some have probably already made landfall. I think it's time you abandon this post and see what you can do to help the agents. Give them your full cooperation. I have a feeling things are about to get messy here in Newport. Let's try and cauterize the wound before it begins to bleed too much."

"Yes sir," the officer said and placed his hand on the butt of his gun. He moved to get into his vehicle when Officer Hassett grabbed the officer's shoulder and made him pause. "If you see anything, you know what to do."

"Yes, I do."

"Very good," Officer Hassett said and returned to his cruiser and moved on to speak to the next officer commanding a post not too far away.

48

LIFETIME DREAM REALIZED

Dr. Hughes watched on in terror and equal excitement at the discovery of the beast. He pressed his binoculars into his face so hard that his eyes watered.

The beast was a killer, motivated by the instinct to survive and to protect its lair. It had to be somewhere near where the attacks were taking place right now.

"Its home is near where it is attacking," Dr. Hughes shouted into the radio. He didn't even know if they could hear him anymore. "Have the frogmen check beneath the surface for an opening."

Dr. Hughes moved the voice recorder close to his mouth and started to speak into it. He watched the monster maneuver around and strategically kill the men and close the circle in which they had to fight back.

"This is Doctor Stephen Hughes. I'm a cryptozoologist, and I am looking at a species never before seen here at the banks of the White River in Newport, Arkansas. The monster I am seeing appears to be around eight feet tall when comparing the size of the head to the people it is in combat with. Primordial, I can see webs on the fingers, spiny rays and dorsal fins on top of the head. I believe I've caught a glimpse of tendrils. I'm hypothesizing that the creature is a crossbreed of fish, amphibian, reptile, and mammal. Truly the first of its kind, and I am astonished and equally frightened by what I see."

Click. Gurgle. Click. Click.

The strange sound stole Dr. Hughes' attention, and he looked down from the rock he stood on. Three creatures looked at him; all had distinct differences including size, color, skull shape, and stature. But clearly, they were of the same breed. One of them held onto the FBI agent he'd had monitoring the perimeter. The agent's body was mangled, and hunks of meat were missing from his torso.

Click.

One monster growled at another. The dead body was dropped, and a mix of fear and accomplishment entered Dr. Hughes' heart. This was what he had spent a lifetime looking for.

Gurgle. Gurgle.

Dr. Hughes watched them, noting that they had a language, and he was mesmerized by being able to see them so close up.

Another emerged from the water.

Click.

Gurgle.

One of the monsters reached out and grabbed Dr. Hughes by his ankle and dragged him off the boulder. He dropped the recorder, and his hat fell off. Both items fell somewhere on the shoreline; the recorder blended into the small river rocks. The river monster grabbed his face with its webbed hand and pulled him close.

"You're cold," Dr. Hughes said, his voice gentle. "And you have a smell about you."

The monster turned Dr. Hughes' face from side to side.

Dr. Hughes' reached a slow, trembling hand up and touched the creature's face. The skin was soft but slimy and had scales. He avoided the teeth and moved his hand upward and felt the spiny rays and dorsal fins. The doctor let his hand slide down the side of the monster's face and he rested his hand on its cheek.

"You're beautiful," he said. "You're all so beautiful."

The pinhole eyes watched his hand a moment more before the monster bit down and amputated the doctor's hand.

"Argh!" Dr. Hughes shouted.

Click. Gurgle.

The monster chewed and then swallowed his hand. It then reached down and picked the doctor up by his waist and lifted him over its head and swung him down. Dr. Stephen Hughes' back was slammed into the boulder, and everything went numb. He wished he could pet it one last time.

Snap.

Death came instantly as Dr. Hughes' spine shattered and the back of his head smashed open and stained the top of the rock. The monster let him go, and the corpse fell to the ground. Strangely, it seemed like the doctor had a smile on his face.

The pack of White River monsters turned their attention to the forest, and they spread out as they advanced toward the men encroaching on their land. Through the Hissters' yard they went and came upon Joan first. She was looking in the opposite direction, smoking a cigarette, seeming oblivious to the things that were going on around her.

Click.

She turned around, and she didn't react either way. She must have gotten a hold of her husband's medication and taken a heavy dose.

Gurgle.

She just stood there, and one of the monsters reached out and grabbed her bottom jaw with one hand and the top with the other. Prying her mouth apart, the bottom jaw was yanked from her face and discarded. She fell to her knees, and a tendril wrapped around her throat and tightened, strangling her to death.

Click. Click.

Gurgle.

Click.

The monsters moved farther into the forest, their formation mimicking that of the trained soldiers they were up against.

49

TURF WAR

"I'm bringing the boat ashore to try and lure them onto the land," Roger said to Marty and sped toward the shoreline. The craft slid onto land in the cutout, and Roger saw Dr. Hughes' pulverized body.

"Oh my God," Roger said, looking away. "We need to fan out, but remain near enough that we can still see each other," he said to his remaining men. "There's strength in numbers, and these things seem to work in groups as well. These creatures are efficient killers, and if we are to survive this, we need to tap into our animal instincts. They obviously came through this way already, so we're going to try and flank them. Let's have a quick ammunition check."

The three men assessed their weapons and ammunition.

"I have two mags plus one in the chamber."

"I'm down to one."

"I down to one, too," Roger said. "Let's conserve our ammo and be precise in our shots. Now let's go."

The men were spaced apart about ten feet. They used hand signals to communicate with each other and went from tree to tree. Every footfall, inhale and exhale of breath was controlled.

Roger pointed at his own eyes, motioned dead ahead, and then closed his fist. The men remained still and looked ahead. A monster knelt on top of a kicking deer, suffocating it and biting into its flesh.

Roger pointed at himself and signaled for the men to cover him. He approached from the rear and took his time, understanding that the things that might be to his left or right were as important as what was going on in front of him. That's the trust he put into his men. When he closed in to about five feet, he raised his gun and aimed it at the head. He tapped the trigger once, and the river monster fell over, dead.

"One down," he whispered. "And that means they can be killed."

Distant, chaotic gunfire drew their attention, and the men hurried to the firefight.

"Stay in formation, men," Roger said, but his guys weren't having any part of it. They were in close quarters combat, and their survival instinct overtook their training. "Damn it," Roger said and tried to keep pace.

Another one of their men was trying to fend off a monster that stood over him and knocked his weapon away with one hand and sent its claws across his face with the other.

They were too far to shoot at the monster without endangering the life of the agent, but panic took over and they shot anyway. Their bullets missed grossly and allowed the creature enough time to descend on the man and mangle him with teeth and claw.

Gurgle.

Roger looked left and saw that two of the river monsters were running toward him, plowing over small trees, their focus on him.

Click. Click.

Roger looked to the right, and he saw that three were coming from that direction.

"We have incoming, guys!"

Roger raised his gun to shoot, but his hands were clumsy and the creatures were closing in fast. He took his chances and ran into the woods and didn't stop running until he was tired and out of breath.

During his attempt to escape, he heard some shots ring out and the finality of what sounded like someone screaming out in torturous pain. He didn't know how many men were still alive, and he didn't want to die that way.

A fat oak tree gave him plenty of cover, and he waited a moment before he looked out from behind the tree.

A river monster was about twenty feet away, and it sniffed the air. That's when one of the FBI agents he was with jumped out from behind a tree and started to shoot at the monster.

"Die, you mother—"

Blam.

The FBI agent crumbled where he stood.

A Newport sheriff's deputy stepped out from behind a tree as he lowered his sidearm. Roger slapped a hand over his mouth and hid behind the tree. His searched for his radio to warn Marty, but it was gone. He was certain he was the last man alive on land. He searched his pockets again but found nothing. The radio had probably dropped when he got out of the boat or when he was running through the woods.

Gurgle. Click. Click.

There were so many of them and only one of him. He asked himself why he kept insisting to Marty that he join him in Arkansas. Now he supposed the reason was simple: He came here to die.

50

CARNAGE

Green-speckled brown skin on webbed, clawed hands grabbed the side of Marty's boat and sliced through the thick rubber. The men tried to shoot into the water but were unable to gain any footing and would be in danger of friendly fire.

On his way into the water, Marty counted at least five creatures. They were instantly on top of his frogmen, devouring them in a pool of flesh and blood. Their screams were muted but not impossible to hear behind the full face mask.

Marty was torn upstream by the current, which worked on submerging him and allowed him back up for only a moment to catch his breath. But he was breathing in water and was unable to hold onto his weapon because he was in a fight to keep his head above the water.

Reaching a hand out in hopes of getting a grip on anything that could slow all this down, a course outcropping of submerged rock allowed him a firm hold. Stopping with a snap, his shoulder hurt instantly. The current pulled on him hard, and he swam behind the rock to reduce the pull.

Once situated, he rested his head for a moment, tired from the sloshing, rushing water that tossed and beat him around as it pleased. Weak and breathing heavy from his fight, he pulled himself on top of the rock and remained as still as he could. The creatures were still feasting on the men who had fallen in.

More and more monsters surfaced and joined in on the feeding frenzy. Marty thought about submitting himself to the current and calling out to the creatures. There was no way he could survive this. Besides, how could he live with himself when he'd cost all of these men their lives?

A frogman surfaced and tried to use the rocks as cover. Marty watched him take aim and shoot one of the monsters. It turned and looked at the frogman and dipped below the water but soon floated to the surface. Unconscious, the creature was being tossed around by the water and headed straight for the rock Marty was hiding behind.

One of the larger, seemingly older monsters scooped up his kin and took him away. Marty placed his head down and sighed his relief as he tried to figure out what options he had at his disposal. He looked at the monsters, and as scary as they were, he was comforted that it would be over quickly if he decided to submit.

51
SURVIVAL OF THE FITTEST

Roger pressed his back against the tree and took a moment to try to understand what he just saw. Why would a Newport police officer shoot an FBI agent engaged with a river monster?

They were protecting the monsters!

Roger shook his head. That was ludicrous.

He moved slowly and looked out from behind the tree. The officer was standing there, his back to Roger, and he was watching the monster drag the agent away.

"The men on land have been all taken care of," the officer said into his radio. "We've got to get Hugh and Johnny and some of the other boys and start to clean this place up, and quick. It looks like a war broke out here."

"10-4," a voice came through the radio.

The officer lit a cigarette and leaned against the tree he stood next to. Roger moved as quietly as possible and located a thick branch. He moved through the forest without making a sound. Anger at what he had seen this man do to one of his comrades gave him the strength to draw the branch back and swing it toward the side of his head.

Crack.

Blood spattered, and the officer fell the same way as the man he had shot. Roger took his pistol and ran in the opposite direction that the monster had gone. Officer Hassett came out from behind a cluster of trees, and the two men collided. Both men crashed to the ground, dazed. They both struggled to find their footing, and by the time they did, they found themselves surrounded by five monsters.

The monsters growled, and one stepped forward, stretched his arms back, looked high into the sky, and let out a primal scream.

Click. Click.

Gurgle.

The creature fell back into formation, and Roger found himself back to back with Officer Hassett. "This is our last stand," Roger said. "Let's take as many of them as we can with us."

Gurgle. Click. Click.

"I would love to do that," Officer Hassett said. "I really would. But they don't want me. They only want you."

Time stopped for Roger when Officer Hassett stepped out of the circle and hesitated as if he was going to say something but changed his mind.

"We have to protect them," Officer Hassett said. "If the world was to know about them, they'd dissect them . . . interfere with the balance of nature here."

The monsters closed the circle and moved in on Roger.

"Hey, Hassett?"

Roger raised the pistol he'd taken off the other officer and got off two quick shots.

Pow. Pow.

He hit Officer Hassett in the neck and head. His blood spray and quick descent to the ground sent the monsters into a frenzy. They grabbed at Roger and knocked the weapon out of his hand. Limb by limb, they tore him apart, arms and legs, and then went for his soft midsection, digging their claws into his stomach and removing his insides until there was nothing but shredded meat and bone left. Then one of the elders stepped in and removed his head and held it up.

52

THE MONSTERS LAIR

A frogman surfaced behind Marty and reached to cover his mouth. Marty turned quickly and was relieved to see it was one of his men.

The diver put a finger up to his lips, and Marty nodded his head in acknowledgment. The diver gave Marty the alternate air source and a tether that was connected to his dive belt. He pointed down to let him know they would be descending.

The frogman counted down from five with his fingers, and when he got to one they dipped beneath the water. Marty was blinded by the strong current and murky water. He held onto the tether with all of his strength. The frogman pulled him along, using the boulders for assistance.

Marty blindly groped his way along until he felt a break in the rocks below the water's surface. The pressure of the river diminished, and the two men began to ascend. When they surfaced, the two men found themselves in a chamber filled with the bones of animals both big and small. A hole high up the mountain allowed daylight to seep inside.

They walked out of the water and onto the hard ground. Human remains were mixed among the bones of animals. Marty found himself looking for something that would indicate that they had taken Ailish here. But there was no making sense of the bones. Some looked like they were newly placed there, while others crumbled to the touch.

The smell was horrible inside the lair of the beasts, and Marty took off his shirt and covered his nose and mouth. The frogman broke a glow stick and tossed it into a shadowed corner. It lit up a small passageway. Marty went there, picked up the glow stick, and held it up high as he moved forward.

He looked inside the chamber and then back at the frogman. He had his weapon aimed at the pool of water puddling where they had entered the labyrinth, keeping post at the entrance while offering Marty a chance to look around inside.

Marty walked in, and the first thing he saw was an altar. Built out of bone, the sturdy configuration was as perfect as if human hands had constructed it.

On top of the altar was Rick Hisster. His head had nearly been severed from the body, and putrefaction made Marty look away. Behind the altar, a pile of bones were stacked over five feet tall. Spanish gold was scattered about the room.

Marty looked up, and on the wall behind the altar and above the bones was a large, strange looking statue, which sat on top of an outcropping of rock. Part octopus, man, and dragon, the mythological deity Cthulhu looked down on his offerings, neither pleased nor displeased that Marty was there.

53

A GREATER PURPOSE

Outside the chamber, Marty heard two gunshots and a man shout out in pain. A skirmish was taking place out there, and Marty knew he didn't have a lot of time left to take in all he was seeing.

Everything went silent, and Marty tossed the glow stick and hid behind the altar as someone walked into the room. Strangely, he sensed that the footsteps were human and not monster.

"You've caused us a great deal of trouble," a woman said. "You sent your agent and her sister here to find her husband and brother-in-law, and like most people who come here seeking the monster, they found much more than they bargained for."

The woman paced in front of the altar.

"All of the agents are dead, and you are the only one left. Soon, any trace of their ever having been here will be erased, and the legend of the White River Monster will return to just being a legend. I want to congratulate you on being the first person to ever make it into the worship chamber alive. Cthulhu is the god of the monsters. Their sacrifices to him are endless, and they need to eat." She paused. "There are other chambers here filled with the remains of people long ago forgotten, and as time goes on, the rooms will continue to be filled, and more people will be forgotten."

Marty stood up and saw an officer of the law dressed in uniform, badge, utility belt, and bulletproof vest. She was holding her sidearm.

"I don't think we've formerly met. I'm Officer Antoinette Ferrara of the Newport Police Department."

The glow stick light played tricks on Marty's eyes. He believed he saw tentacles come out of the sleeve of her clothing on the hand she held the weapon in before the apparition of the appendages retreated.

"This has turned into something so much bigger than we were prepared for," Antoinette said. "You see, you were getting to the truth, and although we thought about killing you, the river monsters didn't want us to. So instead, Officer Hassett and I set Daniel up. The woman he killed was just a visitor in from another state, here to have a good time. She and her family wanted to ride the rapids of the White River. It's a shame what happened, but it's necessary."

Marty looked at the altar, and Rick Hisster's bodily fluids dripped inside of it and pooled on the floor. Marty realized that he was kneeling in them.

"But we had to kill the family and find a way to use her as bait." She raised her hands. "It's not like *we* had to kill the family. We just sent them down the river, and the monsters did the rest. Creating the idea that there was a White River Killer was a plausible explanation to what might have happened to your friend and her family, thus alleviating any suspicion of a legendary creature. But you have that police mentality, and you weren't convinced." She holstered her weapon and paced some more. "Do you know Officer Hassett pulled that woman from the water, hit Daniel in the head with the stick, placed them both in the cutout, and planted the weapons, knowing that when Daniel woke he would snap?"

"No."

"That young man doesn't have the brain capacity to see the way things are. He can't analyze."

"Why are you protecting these monsters?"

She held a finger up. "Hold on. I'm not up to that yet. Did you know I went through the trouble of setting up that campsite to make it look real? A tent, sleeping bag, miscellaneous things around, and even a campfire; what would make you look to the waters?"

"A gut feeling," Marty said. "Years of seeing it all, I guess."

The monsters began to come in behind the officer, and they hissed at Marty.

"Now, now," Antoinette said. "You've had enough blood for a day."

Click. Gurgle. Click. Click.

They all began talking at once, and they dragged the frogman into the room. They broke his limbs, pushed Hisster off the altar, and his body fell at Marty's feet with a heavy thud. They lifted the frogman up and placed him on the altar and bowed as they backed away.

"You're going to need to come out from behind there now," Antoinette said.

Marty stepped around to the front side of the altar, and his eyes watched the untamed beasts. The largest one with the brown skin stepped forward and grabbed Marty's face.

Click. Gurgle.

It looked at Officer Ferrara.

Thock. Thock.

"That's good," she said. "Let's get it over with then."

The creature squeezed Marty's cheeks and forced his mouth open. A tendril slid down his throat, and he started to gag and tried to pull away from the monster, but it was much too strong.

"Don't resist it. The change will take place whether you want it to or not, and it will take place soon enough. Rejoice, for you have been chosen to serve them."

The tendril slid out of Marty's mouth, and he collapsed to the ground and began to choke. He could feel things moving around inside his stomach and throat. He coughed and hacked in an attempt to get them out.

"Welcome, Captain. You'll be instrumental in deflecting any scrutiny away from our legend. You may want to sit, because you will need sleep before the change can take place."

He didn't have time to sit. Darkness descended over Marty, and he staggered forward and flopped face first onto the floor, convulsing.

54

THE CYCLE STARTS OVER

Marty was at the rental shack with Hugh. He was helping him stack some rafts, restock missing helmets and life vests.

"I reckon we'll see two to three rentals a day coming through here," Hugh said. "When we're in season, we don't take them all. Try and remember that."

The breeze blew, and it was beautiful. The smell of the foliage and the fine mist in the air made everything about this place seem perfect.

"I'll do my part," Marty said.

"And I'll do mine, as Officer Ferrara will do her part. So will my nephew. He averages two to three people a week. He drops them off at that little decline beside the riverbank and lets them have a taste of adventure."

"About that," Marty said as he continued to work. "Why are the people dropped off all the way back there if he could drive them up farther?"

"Tire them out. Make them need your help. The Flowers did a pretty good job, but I think you're going to be so much better. You have a friendly face, and you have training. You know how to manipulate people into doing things for you they normally wouldn't. That skill will come into good use."

"Thank you," Marty said, and the sound of a vehicle pulling up stopped their conversation.

"Hello, folks," Hugh said. "Are you looking to ride the White River today?"

"We sure are," a young man said and pulled his girlfriend close.

"Great, let me go over some of the basic things you'll need to know before we set you on your way to having the adventure of a lifetime."

"Marty?" Johnny Phatz said into the radio clipped to Marty's belt.

"Go ahead."

"I just dropped a camper off at the hill."

"10-4, I'm on my way," Marty said.

Hugh outfitted the couple with the safety equipment, asked if they needed a guide, and the two shook their heads.

"I'll need you to sign here," Hugh said, the raft already in the launch area. "Helmets and vests are to stay on during your entire duration in the raft. About five miles down, you will see a station just like this one. You will turn your gear in there, and you'll be shuttled back here."

"Sounds great," the couple said and got into the raft.

"Put your personal items in here," Hugh said and placed an open plastic box in front of them. "You lose it in the river, it's gone forever. Even the keys to your car."

They both stuck their valuables inside the lockbox, and Hugh locked it and fastened the key to the young man's vest. "That way I don't have access to your things."

"This is great!"

They each took their paddles, Hugh gave the raft a shove, and the current took them away. He immediately went into the cage, got the chum, and dumped it into the water.

"They're about to look terror right in the eye," Hugh said.

"Scariest darn thing I've ever seen."

"You better get yourself home so you can intercept the hiker."

"I'm heading out now," Marty said. He jumped into his vehicle and drove to his place. He started busying himself by raking leaves in the yard. Soon, the camper came into view and waved at Marty. Marty waved back, placed the rake down, and approached the hiker.

"What brings you to these parts?"

"I'm on a quest to find out if I can get some evidence of the White River Monster."

Marty laughed, and the man seemed confused. "I'm sorry," Marty said. "If I had a dollar every time someone came through here and said that, I'd be a rich man."

"I've come prepared, and if there is a monster out there, I believe I am capable of capturing it on film. I've brought plenty of gear that's very efficient in the dark."

"So, what's the curiosity driven from? Are you a writer or a reporter or something?"

"No sir, I'm just an enthusiast."

"Well, if you keep heading straight, you're going to come to a break in the trees, and there will be a circular cutout that's perfect to set up camp for the night. If the legend were true, and as people have told me, that is the best spot for you to find the truth you are seeking."

"Thank you."

"You're very welcome."

The man turned away and kept on the path.

"If you don't mind," Marty said, stopping the man with his words. "When you're done, I'd love for you to stop by and tell me what you experienced, if anything. I'm waiting for someone to tell me they've spotted Whitey, and I'm hoping you're him. Maybe I can prep you a good meal to satisfy you during your long hike back."

"That would be great. I think I'll do that."

"If I'm not outside, please stop in and let me know you're back," Marty said and went back to raking leaves.

BOOKS BY
KEITH ROMMEL

Thanatology Series

The Cursed Man

The Lurking Man

The Sinful Man

The Silent Woman

Among the People

Devil Tree Series

The Devil Tree

The Devil Tree II

The White River Monster

Ice Canyon Monster